Caught in the act . . .

Elizabeth paused outside the office door. Painted on the frosted glass window were the words Beaumont Charm School. Elizabeth listened for a moment. No noise came from within, so she stealthily walked into the office.

Elizabeth hurried over to the file cabinet. As soon as she opened one of the drawers she spotted files labeled with familiar names—Fowler, Riteman, Howell, and others. She pulled out the Riteman file and flipped through the contents. The file contained bills of sale for two pieces of furniture and a painting. Then she flipped through the Fowler file and saw the bill for the painting Lila's father had bought.

I've got to find some proof that the things the Beaumonts sold are fakes, Elizabeth thought. But before she could look any further she heard footsteps coming up the stairs from the gallery.

Elizabeth jammed the files back into place and shut the drawer. Suddenly the footsteps were right outside the door. There was no time to escape.

D0369863

Bantam Skylark Books in the SWEET VALLEY TWINS AND FRIENDS series
Ask your bookseller for the books you have missed

SWEET VALLEY TWINS
AND FRIENDS

The Charm School Mystery

◇

Written by
Jamie Suzanne

Created by
FRANCINE PASCAL

A BANTAM SKYLARK BOOK
NEW YORK · TORONTO · LONDON · SYDNEY · AUCKLAND

RL 4, 008–012

THE CHARM SCHOOL MYSTERY
A Bantam Skylark Book / November 1992

*Sweet Valley High® and Sweet Valley Twins and Friends are
trademarks of Francine Pascal*

Conceived by Francine Pascal

*Produced by Daniel Weiss Associates, Inc.
33 West 17th Street
New York, NY 10011*

Cover art by James Mathewuse

*Skylark Books is a registered trademark of Bantam Books, a division of
Bantam Doubleday Dell Publishing Group, Inc.
Registered in U.S. Patent and Trademark Office and elsewhere.*

ISBN 0-553-48050-2

Published simultaneously in the United States and Canada

*Bantam Books are published by Bantam Books, a division of Bantam
Doubleday Dell Publishing Group, Inc. Its trademark, consisting of
the words "Bantam Books" and the portrayal of a rooster, is Registered
in U.S. Patent and Trademark Office and in other countries. Marca
Registrada. Bantam Books, 666 Fifth Avenue, New York, New York
10103*

PRINTED IN THE UNITED STATES OF AMERICA

CWO   0 9 8 7 6 5 4 3 2 1

The
Charm
School
Mystery

One

◇

"Charm school!" Amy Sutton rolled her eyes. "Give me a break. Didn't those things go out of style somewhere around the turn of the century?"

Elizabeth Wakefield giggled. "I guess not."

The two girls were standing in downtown Sweet Valley, reading a poster that had been taped in the front window of the old Swan Lake Dance Studio.

" 'Charm classes conducted by Monique Beaumont of Switzerland,' " Elizabeth read aloud. She pressed her nose against the glass and peered in. "Looks more like an art gallery than a school."

The little bell on the door tinkled and an elegantly dressed woman stepped out. She was very petite and wore her black hair pulled back in a sleek chignon. "I'm sorry," she said in a heavily accented voice. "But the Beaumont Gallery will not open until tomorrow night."

"It's a gallery? Then where's the charm school?" Elizabeth asked.

The woman smiled. "They are both right here. My husband is opening an art and antiques gallery on the first floor. I will use the second-floor studio for a charm school." She extended a well-manicured hand. "My name is Monique Beaumont."

"I'm Elizabeth Wakefield," Elizabeth said politely, shaking the woman's hand. "And this is Amy Sutton."

"My husband and I are from Switzerland," Mrs. Beaumont said. "And we have brought many beautiful things from Europe. We hope that Sweet Valley will learn to appreciate them as we do."

Elizabeth peered in the window again. The building had been empty for a long time, and it didn't look as if the Beaumonts had fixed it up much. But she could see that there were some pretty paintings and furnishings inside.

"We also hope that Sweet Valley will learn to appreciate the art of gracious living," Mrs. Beaumont continued. "That is why I am offering my charm course. Do you girls go to Sweet Valley Middle School?"

"Yes," Amy said.

"Sixth grade," Elizabeth added.

Mrs. Beaumont nodded. "Wonderful. Then perhaps your parents will be receiving an invitation to our gallery reception tomorrow night."

At that moment a white van pulled up and parked on the street in front of the building. A tall, slim young man with a mustache stepped out of it. Elizabeth gave him a friendly smile. "Hi. Are you Mr. Beaumont?"

The man gave her a chilly smile in return. "No. My name is Richard. I work for the Beaumonts." Elizabeth noticed that his accent was slightly different from Mrs. Beaumont's.

"Are you from Switzerland, too?" Elizabeth asked.

"Yes," he answered.

"No," said Mrs. Beaumont at the same time.

They looked at each other.

"No," he answered just as Mrs. Beaumont said, "Yes."

Mrs. Beaumont gave Richard a dirty look. Then she turned to Elizabeth with a tight smile. "When one is European, it is sometimes difficult to be specific about one's origins. Richard was born in France, but raised in Switzerland. You can see that it is confusing."

"I guess," Elizabeth replied. It didn't actually seem all that complicated to her.

Mrs. Beaumont glanced at Richard. "Come, Richard. We have much work to do if the gallery is to open as scheduled." She turned to the girls with a gracious smile. "You must excuse us, my dears. It was a pleasure to meet you, and I look forward to seeing you both in charm class." She gave a graceful little wave and disappeared into the gallery, with Richard right behind her.

"Don't you think that was weird?" Elizabeth asked as she and Amy strolled down the block toward the Dairi Burger.

"Don't I think what was weird?"

"That stuff about where Richard is from."

Amy shrugged. "I wasn't really paying much attention. I was too busy thinking about the triple-scoop hot-fudge-and-banana sundae I'm going to get at the Dairi Burger." She pulled Elizabeth through the door of the crowded restaurant.

"Elizabeth, over here," a voice called out.

Elizabeth's identical twin sister, Jessica, was sitting in a booth with her friends Janet Howell, Lila Fowler, and Kimberly Haver.

"Are we interrupting an official Unicorn meeting or anything?" Elizabeth asked as she and Amy sat down. Jessica, Lila, Janet, and Kimberly were all members of the Unicorn Club, a group of the prettiest and most popular girls in Sweet Valley

Middle School. Elizabeth loved her twin more than anyone else in the world, but she wasn't crazy about her friends. As far as she could tell, the Unicorns' interests were limited to clothes, parties, gossip, boys, and themselves. Their official club color was purple, the color of royalty, and each member tried to wear something purple every day.

Elizabeth's interests were very different from her sister's. She enjoyed writing for *The Sweet Valley Sixers*, the sixth-grade newspaper she had helped to start. Elizabeth wanted to be a writer when she grew up. When she wasn't working on an article for the paper, Elizabeth liked to curl up with a good book. Her favorite writer was Amanda Howard, who wrote mysteries featuring a clever young detective named Christine Davenport. Elizabeth had read every one of her books.

Sometimes it was difficult for people to believe how different Elizabeth and Jessica really were, because on the outside they looked exactly alike. Both girls had blue-green eyes, long blond hair, and a dimple.

"No, we're not having a meeting," Jessica told her twin. "We were just talking about the new charm school."

"I think it's ridiculous," Kimberly said. "Charm schools are real geek factories. Besides, the Unicorns are charming enough."

Lila shook her head. "You're way off, Kimberly. My cousin in New York has a friend who went to charm school in Europe—only they called it a finishing school. Anyway, she wound up marrying a duke."

"I see what you're getting at, Lila," Janet said thoughtfully. Janet was an eighth grader and the president of the Unicorns. "Maybe the idea isn't so silly after all. The Unicorns are sort of like the royalty of Sweet Valley Middle School. Maybe it *would* be a good idea to get a little polish."

"But they might not let us in," Kimberly pointed out. "Caroline Pearce told me she talked to that Swiss guy, Richard, who works for the Beaumonts. He told her the Beaumonts are inviting only a few select people to this reception tomorrow night. They want to look the families over before they let their daughters into the charm school. Richard told Caroline that's the way they do it in Grenoble, where he grew up." Kimberly said *Grenoble* in an exaggerated French accent.

"He said he grew up in Grenoble?" Elizabeth asked with a frown. "That's strange. I'm pretty sure Grenoble is in France, not Switzerland."

"Who cares?" Jessica said impatiently. "The important thing is whether we'll get invitations."

Janet lifted her chin. "Well, I'm sure I'll be getting one. The Howells are one of the most important families in Sweet Valley."

Lila gave Janet an irritated look. "I'm sure I'll get one, too," she said. "After all, my father is—" Lila bit her lip. Just a few weeks earlier, Lila had been afraid that her father, one of the wealthiest people in Sweet Valley, had lost all his money. The experience had made Lila a little more sensitive to people who weren't as privileged as she was. "Pretty important, too," she finished quietly.

"And the richest man in town," Amy added with a laugh.

Lila shrugged. "Well, in any case, I'm expecting my invitation to be one of the first to arrive." She tossed her light brown hair over her shoulder. "It wouldn't be a reception without me."

Jessica frowned. "I'm sure Lizzie and I will get an invitation, too. Our father is a very important lawyer and our mom is a well-known interior designer. They're definitely somebody in this town."

Elizabeth felt Amy tugging on her sleeve.

"Come on, Elizabeth. Let's hurry up and eat. We've got a *Sixers* meeting in a few minutes."

"I'll see you guys later," Elizabeth said, getting up to follow Amy. "I don't remember any *Sixers* meeting today," she said to her friend when they were safely out of earshot.

"There isn't one," Amy said. "I just couldn't listen to the Unicorns' bragging for another second. It was ruining my appetite."

Elizabeth giggled. "I suspected as much." She shifted her backpack and a book fell out. It hit Amy's toe with a thud.

"Ouch!" Amy yelped. Then she leaned over and picked up the book. *"The Case of the Missing Briefcase,"* she read. *"Another* Amanda Howard book? I thought you'd read all of them at least three times already," Amy teased. "Don't you ever get enough of those mysteries?"

"I can't help it," Elizabeth said. "I'm a mystery addict. I think Amanda Howard's hero, Christine Davenport, is great. She isn't that much older than we are, and she's already solved dozens of mysteries."

"Of course. She's got time. Christine Davenport is a fictional character who never has any homework."

Elizabeth laughed. "Well, I still think she's wonderful. Although I must admit, she does make me feel a little inadequate. I mean, I can't even solve the case of the missing blue sweater."

"If you mean your blue sweater with the white collar, I can solve that mystery for you right now," Amy offered. "I saw Jessica wearing it in here yesterday afternoon."

Elizabeth's eyes narrowed with annoyance. "I can't believe her. I asked her this morning if she'd seen it and she said she hadn't."

"Maybe that's because when I saw her wearing it, she was also wearing half of her strawberry shake," Amy said with a wry grin.

As soon as she got home Elizabeth hurried upstairs to search Jessica's room. The first place she looked was under the bed—and sure enough, she immediately spotted the blue sweater, complete with strawberry-shake stain.

She grabbed the evidence and hurried down the stairs. "Jessica!" she shouted.

She found her twin in the front hall, busily talking on the phone. Jessica waved Elizabeth away impatiently.

"Lila got one. And Janet got one," Jessica was saying, "but we haven't gotten one yet. I'll call you back as soon as we do."

Jessica slammed the phone down. "It's really insulting," she said angrily. "The Howells and the

Fowlers both got hand-delivered invitations to the Beaumonts' reception. They're sure taking their time with ours!"

Elizabeth held up the sweater. "I thought you said you hadn't seen this," she said.

Jessica looked at Elizabeth with round, innocent eyes. "You mean *that* blue sweater? I thought you meant your other blue sweater."

"Jessica!"

Mrs. Wakefield came out of the den in time to hear the end of the conversation. "Jessica, I've told you not to take Elizabeth's clothes without asking her."

As Jessica opened her mouth to respond the doorbell rang. Jessica bounded toward the front door and flung it open. She smiled when she saw the messenger standing outside. "It's here!" she cried triumphantly.

"Letter for Mr. and Mrs. Wakefield," the messenger said.

"I'll take it," Jessica snatched the envelope from the messenger's hand and slammed the door in his face. Then she slit open the envelope with her fingernail.

"Hold it right there," Mrs. Wakefield scolded. "Where are your manners, Jessica?" She removed the envelope from her daughter's hand. Then she opened the door and politely thanked the bewildered messenger.

When Mrs. Wakefield had closed the door again, she turned to Jessica. "I know you know how to say please and thank you. I also thought you knew better than to open mail that's not addressed to you."

"Sorry, Mom," Jessica said, eying the envelope. "But I know what it is. It's an invitation to the charm school reception tomorrow night at the Beaumont Gallery. You're supposed to bring me and Elizabeth. We have to go. We just have to. Please say yes."

Mrs. Wakefield opened the envelope and scanned the invitation. "Oh, yes," she said thoughtfully. "I did hear something about the Beaumonts. They're supposed to have a lot of wonderful antiques and art to sell."

"So will you take us?" Jessica asked eagerly.

"Count me out," Elizabeth said. "I think charm school is silly."

"Well, I *would* like to take a look at some of the things in the gallery," Mrs. Wakefield said. She was a part-time interior designer, so she was always interested in looking at art and furnishings. "But what's this business about charm school?"

"Mrs. Beaumont is opening a charm school in the studio above the gallery," Jessica explained. "All the Unicorns want to go."

Mrs. Wakefield glanced at the invitation again. "Well, if you really want to go to charm school, I suppose there's no reason you shouldn't."

The words were barely out of her mouth when Jessica jumped up and grabbed the phone. "All right!" she exclaimed. "I've got to call Lila and tell her the good news."

Mrs. Wakefield smiled at Jessica. "The way you've been acting lately," she said, "a little refresher course in good manners might not be a bad idea."

Two

◇

"What do you think of this one?" Jessica asked, twirling into Elizabeth's room in a short lavender skirt and an ivory sweater. She turned around slowly, imitating a fashion model.

"How many outfits are you going to try on?" Elizabeth asked impatiently. She was sitting on her bed, trying to read her Amanda Howard mystery. "I'm getting tired of being your fashion consultant."

"Just one more," Jessica promised, disappearing into her room.

A moment later she was back, this time wearing a deep violet blouse. "What do you think?"

"That looks great," Elizabeth said.

Jessica pulled a skirt out of Elizabeth's closet. "Actually, what would you think of this combination?" She held up the skirt so that Elizabeth could see how it looked with the violet blouse.

"Everything you've put on looks fine," Elizabeth said. "What's the big deal, anyway? It's a reception at an art gallery, not dinner at the White House."

"But I'll bet it's really elegant," Jessica said. "I want to be sure I look . . . well . . . charming." She grabbed a filmy white scarf off Elizabeth's dresser and draped it over her shoulders. Then she carefully examined her reflection in the mirror.

Elizabeth laughed. "I don't care what you wear. But if it belongs to me, just be sure you don't spill anything on it or stash it under your bed."

"Jessica! Elizabeth! Dinner," they heard their mother call.

Jessica and Elizabeth ran down the stairs and took their places at the dinner table, where Mr. and Mrs. Wakefield and Steven, the twins' fourteen-year-old brother, were already seated.

Steven reached over and grabbed the scarf from around Jessica's shoulders and tied it around his head like a bandana. "How's this?" he asked. "Do I look like a charm school graduate or what?"

Jessica stuck out her tongue at him. "The only thing you'd pass for is an idiot-school graduate."

Steven turned to Elizabeth. "So why aren't

you all dolled up, dahling?" he asked, fluttering his eyelashes at her.

"Because I'm not going," she replied. "Amy's coming over after dinner to spend the night."

"Why, wasn't Amy invited to the reception?" Steven teased. "Is she already charming? Or just a hopeless case?"

"She was invited. She just doesn't want to go," Elizabeth said. She turned to her parents. "But some girls weren't invited. Melissa McCormick wasn't, and neither was Sophia Rizzo. And Jessica says that Mandy Miller wasn't, either."

"That's odd," Mrs. Wakefield commented. "I would have thought they'd invite all the girls."

Elizabeth nodded. "Me, too. It's kind of weird."

"Well, I think you're smart to stay away from charm school, Elizabeth," Steven said, stuffing a huge forkful of mashed potatoes into his mouth. "I'm just glad I have basketball practice tonight so you can't try to drag me along."

"Oh, yeah, like we'd want you there anyway," Jessica snapped. "And don't talk with your mouth full."

Mr. Wakefield gave Jessica and Steven a warning look. "Actually, I think I'll tag along to the reception tonight," he said. "Elizabeth and Amy will be all right on their own for a couple of hours, and I wouldn't mind seeing the antiques and the art."

Jessica gazed at her father doubtfully. "Just don't make fun of the charm school, OK? And don't say anything grosh."

"Grosh?" repeated Mr. Wakefield, looking puzzled.

Mrs. Wakefield laughed. "You mean gauche?"

"That's it," Jessica confirmed.

Mr. Wakefield shook his head. "Get thee to a charm school, Jessica."

Steven took the scarf off his head and tossed it at Jessica. "You guys aren't really going to let Jessica sign up for some crummy charm school, are you?"

"Well, it can't hurt and it might help," Mrs. Wakefield said. "It's only five classes over two and a half weeks." She smiled. "When I was Jessica's age, all the girls in my class were given a course in charm, too. Of course, times were different then. We were all taught how to comb our hair into beehives because that was considered very chic."

Mr. Wakefield gave a mock shudder. "I hope I never see another hairdo like that again."

Mr. and Mrs. Wakefield and Jessica left immediately after dinner. A few minutes later, Steven grabbed his basketball and a handful of cookies and dashed out the door.

Elizabeth locked the front door and then curled up on the couch with her Amanda Howard mystery.

It was dark in the hallway, Elizabeth read. *Christine crept through the empty house, making her way carefully toward the library. The old house had been deserted for twenty years. There wasn't a sound except for the howling of the wind outside. Suddenly—*

Ding dong!

Elizabeth jumped, then let out a sigh of relief. It was just the doorbell. Chuckling at her own jumpiness, she ran to the door to let Amy in.

"Still reading Amanda Howard, I see," Amy observed. "Whodunit?"

"I haven't figured it out yet," Elizabeth said. "Come on in. We've got the house to ourselves for a couple of hours. Mom and Dad took Jessica to the Beaumonts' reception and Steven's at basketball practice."

Amy dropped her overnight bag in the hall. "Great. What kind of trouble can we get into?"

Elizabeth pursed her lips thoughtfully. "Hmm. Let's see. It's a little late to plan a wild party."

"Bummer," Amy said, grinning. "What's plan B?"

"Actually, I do have a plan," Elizabeth said

with a mischievous smile. "My mom said tonight at dinner that when she went to charm school, they taught the girls to comb their hair into these horrible beehive hairdos. Let's do our hair that way and surprise them when they get back."

Amy raised her eyebrows doubtfully and fingered a strand of her limp blond hair. "I don't know, Elizabeth. . . ."

"Come on, it'll be fun," Elizabeth coaxed. "Where's your sense of adventure?"

Amy shrugged. "Well, OK. As long as I don't have to appear in public."

"You won't," Elizabeth promised. She led her friend upstairs to the bathroom that she and Jessica shared. The two girls quickly located a comb, a can of hairspray, and a bunch of bobby pins.

"One more thing," Elizabeth said. She raced downstairs, then came running back with one of her mother's dusty old high school yearbooks. She flipped through it as Amy looked over her shoulder. "Yuck," Elizabeth said. "Look at these hairdos. They're hideous."

"Do you know what year your mom was?" Amy asked.

"Wait a minute," Elizabeth said suddenly, not answering her friend's question. She turned the book back a page. "Look. Do you see what I see?"

"I see a couple of outfits that I wouldn't be caught dead in," Amy replied.

"No, no, look at this girl," Elizabeth said, pointing to one of the photographs. "Doesn't she look like Mrs. Beaumont?"

Amy stared at the old photograph. "Sort of," she said. "But that's not Monique Beaumont. That's . . ." Amy located the corresponding name. "That's Margaret Rudenthaler."

"It looks just like Monique Beaumont to me," Elizabeth insisted. "Look, she was two years behind my mother. I wonder why she's calling herself Monique Beaumont now. And why is she pretending to be Swiss?"

Amy rolled her eyes. "Lots of people look alike. It doesn't mean it's time to start playing Christine Davenport." She handed Elizabeth a comb. "Now quit sleuthing and start teasing."

Jessica was having a terrific time at the Beaumonts' reception. Most of the Unicorns were there, along with lots of other girls from school. Mrs. Beaumont had made a short presentation about the charm school, and then she had invited the guests to have a glass of punch and roam around the gallery.

"Their collection is quite small," Mrs. Wakefield commented to Jessica and Mr. Wakefield. "But what they have looks lovely."

Just then Jessica spotted Mrs. Beaumont on the other side of the room. "I'll be right back," she told her parents. Then she hurried across the room. "Hi, Mrs. Beaumont," she said.

Mrs. Beaumont turned. "Oh, hello," she said with a polite smile. "You are in the sixth grade, yes? And your name is . . . ?"

"Jessica Wakefield," Jessica replied. "I just wanted to tell you I think this charm school is a great idea."

"Well, thank you," Mrs. Beaumont said. "Not that the young ladies of Sweet Valley appear to be lacking in charm."

"Thank you. You're too kind," Jessica said, hoping that was the correct response. "So," she continued, "I'll bet you've met lots of famous people, living in Europe and all."

"Well, yes," Mrs. Beaumont said. "One or two."

"Any kings or queens?" Jessica asked eagerly.

Mrs. Beaumont laughed. "Are you interested in royalty?"

"I sort of always wanted to be a princess," Jessica admitted. Once it was out of her mouth, she was worried it sounded silly.

Mrs. Beaumont gave Jessica a charming

smile. "You are certainly pretty enough to be a princess."

Jessica grinned modestly. "I think so, too," she agreed, hoping she didn't sound as if she was bragging.

But Mrs. Beaumont gave her an approving nod. "It's nice to see a young lady with self-confidence."

"Oh, I have lots of that," Jessica said. "Being a Unicorn makes you very self-confident."

"Unicorn?" Mrs. Beaumont repeated, looking curious.

Jessica told her about the Unicorns, making sure to mention that they were the prettiest and most popular girls in Sweet Valley Middle School.

Mrs. Beaumont looked very interested. "That is good," she said. "If one aspires to move in the first circles, it is important to be discriminating in the matter of one's friends."

Jessica nodded. "I know exactly what you mean."

Mrs. Beaumont lowered her voice to a whisper. "That is why we are being very careful about whom we invite to take part in our charm school. You have perhaps noticed that not all the girls from your school were invited to our reception tonight."

"I did notice," Jessica whispered. "Actually, I was wondering about that."

Mrs. Beaumont put her hand on Jessica's arm, gripping it just a little too tightly. She leaned even closer. "We didn't want just anybody."

Jessica felt a little uncomfortable. But at the same time it was sort of flattering, the way Mrs. Beaumont was confiding in her.

Mrs. Beaumont looked around the room. "On the other hand," she said, "we don't want to exclude any girl who might be . . . well . . . eligible." She pulled a typed list of names from her pocket. "I wonder if you would be good enough to look this over. These are the names of the girls we have invited. Perhaps there are girls we didn't know about. Girls whose parents are . . ." Mrs. Beaumont broke off. "Girls of good background," she finished.

But Jessica had a feeling she knew what Mrs. Beaumont meant. And she suddenly understood why Melissa McCormick and Mandy Miller and Sophia Rizzo had not been invited. Their parents didn't have much money.

It was pretty snobby, and for a moment Jessica felt guilty. Mandy was a good friend and a fellow Unicorn. But then again, Jessica comforted herself, Mandy's parents probably wouldn't have the extra money to send her to charm school anyway, so what was the point of getting her all excited about it? And as for Melissa and Sophia, well, they were hardly charm school material. Jessica ran her eye down the list. "You might want to ask Brooke Dennis and Sarah Thomas. Brooke's dad is a really important screenwriter and her mom is Coco—you know the famous rock star. And Sarah's dad . . . well, I'm not sure what he does, but they live in a really nice house."

Mrs. Beaumont's eyes gleamed. She pulled a pen from her pocket and added the names to the list. "We'll contact their parents," she promised. "You've been very helpful, Jessica. I hope we'll see you in our charm school."

"Oh, you definitely will," Jessica said with a smile.

"What have you done to your hair?" Jessica shrieked as soon as she walked into the living room that evening.

Mr. and Mrs. Wakefield walked in behind her, took one look at Elizabeth and Amy, and began to laugh. Elizabeth and Amy gave them wide-eyed looks of bewilderment.

"What's so funny?" Elizabeth asked with a perfectly straight face. Then she patted her hair, which she had teased into a tall cone that sat like a dunce cap on top of her head.

Amy touched her own hairdo. "We're thinking of starting our own charm school," she said.

"For your information," Jessica said haughtily, "that's not what they teach you in charm school."

Elizabeth grabbed the yearbook from the coffee table and followed her mother into the kitchen with Amy close behind her. "Mom," she said, "do you remember Margaret Rudenthaler?"

Mrs. Wakefield was already busy looking through a pile of mail on the kitchen table. "No," she replied absently. "Do I know her?"

Elizabeth handed her mother the old yearbook. "That's her there," she said, pointing to the picture.

Mrs. Wakefield examined the picture. "Oh, yes," she said. "I vaguely remember her. I don't think she stayed long—maybe a semester."

"Doesn't she look like Mrs. Beaumont?" Elizabeth said.

Mrs. Wakefield frowned. "Yes," she said hesitantly. "I do see a resemblance." She turned her attention back to the papers on the table. "Let's see now," she said to herself. "I know the phone bill was in this pile. . . ."

"*Mom!*" cried Elizabeth. "Don't you think it's weird?"

Amy grabbed her arm. "Come on, Christine

Davenport. Let's go comb this stuff out. I think the weight's doing something to your brain."

Elizabeth sighed. "But there's something strange going on with the Beaumonts. I have a feeling I'm on to a mystery."

"The only mystery I'm worried about right now," Amy said, "is how we're going to get all this gook out of our hair!"

Three

"So is Jessica signing up for charm school?" Maria Slater asked Elizabeth.

It was Monday, and Maria, Elizabeth, and Amy were sitting in the cafeteria splitting a huge piece of chocolate cake.

"Of course," Elizabeth said. "What about you? Jessica said she saw you there with your mom and your sister."

Maria grinned. "Yeah. But Mom thinks charm school is pretentious. She said it's exactly the sort of thing we left Hollywood to get away from. We only went to the reception for the free food."

Elizabeth laughed. When Maria was younger she had been a child star in Hollywood, but she'd gotten too old to play cute little children and was not yet old enough for the really good teenage parts. So her parents had decided to bring her and her sister to Sweet Valley to live a more normal life than they could in Hollywood. Maria missed acting, but she was enjoying going to a real school rather than having a tutor on the movie set. And she especially enjoyed having real friends instead of just co-stars and fans.

"My sister had fun talking to Mrs. Beaumont, though," Maria continued. "She got a chance to practice her French."

Maria's sister, Nina, was in high school and an ace French student. She wanted to be a diplomat or a foreign-service officer when she grew up.

Elizabeth glanced at Amy. "So Mrs. Beaumont really speaks French?" she asked Maria.

Maria gave Elizabeth a puzzled look. "Sure she really speaks French. Why wouldn't she?"

Elizabeth leaned forward. "Because I think she may not be French."

Maria leaned forward, too. "You're right," she whispered, trying to keep a straight face. "She's Swiss." Then she turned to Amy. "What is she talking about?"

"She thinks she's stumbled onto a mystery," Amy replied dryly. "Let's ignore it and hope it goes away."

Maria laughed. "Well, Nina *did* say that Mrs. Beaumont's accent was odd."

"Ah-hah," Elizabeth said, slapping her palm on the table. "I knew it!"

"That's because she's Swiss," Maria explained. "It makes sense that her accent would be different."

Elizabeth's face fell. "Darn," she muttered. "But there *is* something fishy going on. I just know it."

"What makes you think so?"

Elizabeth told Maria about the picture she had found in the yearbook and Richard's confusion about where he was from.

"Hmm," Maria said. "It's not much to go on, is it?"

Elizabeth tapped her nose. "But something smells a little funny."

"Right again, Inspector," Amy said with a giggle. She pointed to the remains of Elizabeth's lunch. "But I'm afraid it's just your corned beef and cabbage."

That evening, Elizabeth sat at one end of the sofa reading her mystery book. Her father sat at the other end reading the newspaper.

Christine opened the drawer, Elizabeth read. *She stared down at the mound of paper and junk scattered inside. Somewhere in that pile, she knew, was the answer to the mystery.*

"Ahem. Ahem."

Mr. Wakefield cleared his throat and turned the page of his newspaper. The pages rattled loudly, and Elizabeth couldn't help wishing he'd quiet down or go into the den to read.

Christine racked her brains. The answer was right in front of her, she was certain. But what was it? Someone had wanted the contents of that drawer badly enough to kill for them. What had he or she been after?

"Ahem! Ahem!"

Rattle. Rattle. Rattle.

Elizabeth sighed. It was impossible to concentrate with all this racket. She glanced at her father and debated whether or not to move up to her room.

Mr. Wakefield turned another page of the newspaper. Suddenly Elizabeth spotted something that made her eyes widen. On the page facing her was a big, bold headline: "Fabulous Fakes: Con Artists Flood Market with Phony Antiques and Art."

Elizabeth drew in her breath with a gasp. It was just like in her book. The answer to the mystery was right in front of her eyes.

Without thinking, Elizabeth reached over and snatched the paper out of her father's hands. "Hey!" he cried in surprise.

"Sorry, Dad," Elizabeth said as she scanned

the article. "But I think I'm on to something. Look at this article." She waved the paper in her father's face. "See? I knew something about the Beaumonts didn't add up. This has got to be it. They're con artists. They're selling phony art and antiques right here in Sweet Valley."

Mr. Wakefield laughed and took the paper from Elizabeth's hands. "Listen, Detective Wakefield, the Beaumonts are ordinary businesspeople. You could get yourself into a lot of trouble spreading rumors like that about them. So as your lawyer—and your father—I'm telling you not to let your imagination run away with you."

Elizabeth sighed in frustration. She knew she was on to something. She just knew it. But how was she going to prove it?

Maria shook her head. "Don't you think you're letting your imagination run away with you?"

"That's what my dad said," Elizabeth replied. "But I'm sure I'm right. All I have to do is prove it."

"How are you going to do that?" Amy asked skeptically.

"By going under cover," Elizabeth announced. "We'll sign up for charm school. Once we get inside their operation, we can start looking for the proof."

Maria's eyes lit up. "You know, that might be kind of fun, even if there's no mystery to solve. It'd be sort of like an acting-school exercise."

Amy shrugged. "Well, I hate to miss out on the action. If you guys are in, I guess I'm in, too. But there's one problem."

"Problem?" Elizabeth said. "What problem? It's the perfect plan."

"My mom was considering trying to talk me into charm school, but then she decided it was too expensive," Amy said. "And Maria's mom thinks it's pretentious. And Elizabeth, you've gone on record as saying you wouldn't be caught dead in charm school. If you change your tune now, your parents will wonder what's going on. So how are we going to convince our parents to let us sign up?"

Elizabeth frowned, thinking hard. Then she broke into a wide grin. "I've got an idea."

Four

That night, Amy came into the dining room just as her mother was setting the table. "Oh," Amy exclaimed. "We're using Great-grandma's china!"

Mrs. Sutton lovingly put one of the delicate plates on the table. "I love to use these old things once in a while," she said. "They're so beautiful and fragile. Someday they'll be yours."

Amy carefully calculated the distance between where she stood and the table. "Let me help," she offered. Then, instead of stepping forward, she pretended to catch her foot in the rug. "Whoops!" she cried.

"Watch out!" Mrs. Sutton shouted.

Amy stumbled again but managed to steady herself just before she would have fallen into the table. "Whew!" she exclaimed. "That was a close one."

Mrs. Sutton let out a long sigh of relief. "Be careful, Amy. You almost knocked all this china right off the table."

Amy's father came out of the kitchen. "I'll help your mother," he said. "Why don't you take out the garbage?"

"Sure," Amy said, heading for the kitchen. But as she did she caught her foot in the leg of a chair, fell forward toward the window, and clutched at the curtains for support.

"Amy!" Mrs. Sutton shrieked.

"Watch out!" Mr. Sutton shouted.

The aluminum curtain rod bounced off Amy's head and then clattered across the floor. The next thing she knew, she was buried under several yards of sheer, lacy fabric.

"Are you all right?" Mr. Sutton asked, helping her up.

"Sure." Amy smiled. "I don't know what's gotten into me. I'm just so clumsy these days. Maybe this is that awkward age people are always talking about."

Mrs. Sutton smiled reassuringly and pushed the curtains out of the way. "You can take the garbage out later, dear. It's time for dinner, anyway. Go ahead and sit down."

During dinner, Amy fell out of her chair twice—once when she reached for the butter, and again when she tried to cut a tough piece of meat. Amy was rather clumsy to begin with, so with a little extra effort she was hopeless.

After dinner Amy helped her mother and father clear the table. But on her way back from the sink, she tripped and stumbled into the broom closet.

The broom closet door banged shut so hard that it shook the wall. The kitchen clock fell from its hook and shattered on the floor.

Mr. Sutton opened the closet door and peered anxiously inside. "Amy?"

Amy pushed aside the mops and brooms that had fallen on top of her. "I'm OK," she reassured him.

"Amy," her mother said, a note of desperation creeping into her voice, "we'll finish cleaning up. Why don't you just sit quietly in the living room?"

"But Mom—"

"*Please!*"

"Well," Amy said sadly, "OK. If that's what you want."

Amy walked out of the kitchen, through the dining room, and into the living room—where she tripped over the coffee table and upset the jigsaw puzzle that her father had been working on for the last two weeks.

"Yeow!" she cried, falling to the floor in a shower of colorful puzzle pieces.

"That does it!" Mr. Sutton shouted in frustration. "I don't care what it costs. She's going to that charm school, like it or not!"

Amy bent her head to hide the triumphant smile on her face.

"It was so nice of you to invite me to dinner," said Ms. Tuckman. "I can't tell you how tired I get of eating in restaurants when I'm traveling on business."

Mrs. Slater smiled. "I'm glad you were able to join us," she said graciously. "I've been wanting you to meet my girls."

Ms. Tuckman was Mrs. Slater's most important client from New York. And Mrs. Slater had warned both Maria and Nina to be on their best behavior.

Ms. Tuckman turned to Maria with a smile. "I understand you're an actress."

Maria took a big bite of her roll. "Ommmph, yes," she said with her mouth full. "I'm werry ex . . . ommmph . . . cited about . . . getting back . . . ommmph . . . into television when I get out of . . . ssssssschool." When Maria hit the *s* in *school*, little bits of food came spraying out of her mouth.

Out of the corner of her eye, Maria could see her mother giving her a horrified look. But Maria kept her attention on Ms. Tuckman, whose smile was beginning to look a little strained. "How very interesting," she said faintly.

Maria took a big swig of her milk and washed down what was left of her roll with a loud gulp.

Ms. Tuckman turned to Nina. "What about you, Nina? Are you interested in—" But before she could finish her sentence, Maria's arm shot out across Ms. Tuckman's plate and grabbed the salt shaker. The move was so sudden that everyone jumped and the plates and silverware rattled on the table.

"Maria!" Mrs. Slater said in surprise. "Where are your manners?"

"Sorry, Mom," Maria grunted, vigorously salting her potatoes.

"We have a guest, dear," Mrs. Slater reminded her gently.

Maria glanced up with a stricken look on her face. "Oh!" she breathed. "I'm so sorry," she said sweetly to Ms. Tuckman. Then she very politely began to salt the food on Ms. Tuckman's plate.

"*Maria!*" her mother and sister exclaimed in unison.

Maria looked from one to the other with wide and bewildered eyes. "What?"

"I don't believe I care for any salt," Ms. Tuckman said in a tight voice.

"I can fix that," Maria said agreeably. She leaned over and blew on Ms. Tuckman's food, trying to blow some of the salt off.

Mrs. Slater stared at her daughter in stunned surprise.

"That's not necessary," snapped Ms. Tuckman, pulling her plate away. Then she took a deep breath and forced a polite smile back onto her face. She turned to Mrs. Slater. "Do your girls have any extracurricular activities?"

Mrs. Slater pursed her lips. "Nina enjoys team sports," she said grimly. "And Maria . . ." She stared at her younger daughter as if she had turned into a monster. "Maria is going to be starting charm school next week."

"Still planning to go to that silly charm school?" Elizabeth asked Jessica that evening at dinner.

"What's so silly about it?" Jessica demanded.

"It's just dumb, that's all," Elizabeth replied haughtily.

"Elizabeth," Mrs. Wakefield scolded. "I'm surprised at you. You should know that just because you're not interested in something doesn't give you the right to put it down."

"Even if it *is* dumb," Steven put in.

"Steven," Mrs. Wakefield said warningly. "Don't tease your sister."

"Yeah, Steven," Jessica said, pleased to have her mother on her side for once. "And besides, it's not dumb. There's room for improvement in everybody—even you, Elizabeth."

Elizabeth looked thoughtful for a moment, but then she shook her head. "No, I don't think so. Charm school may be all right for you Unicorns—I mean, you guys actually care about how to put on makeup and stuff like that." She waved her hand airily. "I don't need that kind of school. If you can call it that."

Jessica glared at her sister. "For your information, Miss Smartypants, there's a lot more to charm school than putting on makeup. Stuff even you might need to know. It's important for everyone to learn things like manners and poise and grooming. Not just for social reasons, but for public speaking and that kind of thing. For instance, if you were running for school president or going to a debate tournament, you'd want to project a confident and well-groomed appearance. Right?"

"That's true," agreed Elizabeth. "I hadn't thought of it that way."

"And the cultural appreciation part of it is very important. I mean, shouldn't everybody know something about art, and furniture, and good taste?"

"They should." Elizabeth nodded. "You know, Jessica, I'm beginning to think that you were right and I was wrong. Maybe I should go to charm school after all."

Jessica's jaw dropped in surprise, but she recovered quickly. "You're all witnesses," she said, pointing to each person at the table with her fork. "Put it on the calendar. Today Elizabeth Wakefield actually admitted that she, Elizabeth, was wrong, and I, Jessica, was right."

Elizabeth shrugged and smiled. "I guess I sounded pretty arrogant—like I thought I was already perfect and didn't have anything to learn." She looked at her parents. "Would it be OK if I went to charm school, too?"

Mrs. Wakefield glanced at her husband. "I suppose so," she said. "We can hardly tell Jessica yes and you no."

"Thanks." Elizabeth smiled. *Look out, Beaumonts*, she thought. *Here I come!*

Five

◇

"Mesdemoiselles! Attention!"

It was Wednesday afternoon, the first day of charm school. The students were gathered in the studio over the Beaumont Gallery, giggling and talking as they waited for class to begin.

"Mesdemoiselles! Please. I need your attention," Mrs. Beaumont said again. She clapped her hands until the girls quieted down.

"I'm delighted to see so many lovely young ladies here today," she began when she finally had their attention. "I know you all will work very hard and make your parents proud. We have a lot to do and a lot to learn. And at the end of the course, you will have a chance to demonstrate what you have learned at our formal graduation ceremony, which will include a seated dinner to which parents and siblings are invited. At that time we will award the Mademoiselle Manners Award."

Mrs. Beaumont walked over to a battered old desk in the corner and produced a glittering tiara from one of the drawers. "The winner of the award will be crowned our Queen of Charm. Since I hope you all will meet many kings and queens someday, we will learn how to behave in the presence of royalty. On the night of our dinner, you all will curtsy to the Queen of Charm, showing your parents that if you ever are invited to tea at Buckingham Palace, you will know what to do."

Most of the girls giggled. But Jessica glanced around at her fellow Unicorns. She knew that they could be very competitive—especially when it came to awards. But in her mind, Jessica was already picturing herself wearing that crown. "I'm going to win that award," she announced to Lila.

Janet, who was seated just behind Lila, heard what Jessica said. "If anybody's going to win," Janet whispered, "it's going to be me. After all, I *am* president of the Unicorns."

Jessica tossed her head. "That doesn't mean anything."

"Wanna bet?" Janet hissed. "Name your terms."

"If I win," Jessica whispered, "you have to

curtsy to me every time you see me for a week. If you win, I have to curtsy to you."

The other Unicorns, who had been listening, giggled and nudged each other.

Mrs. Beaumont frowned in their direction and they fell silent. "Please pay attention," she said sternly. "We have a lot to do." She lifted her chin. "As you know, we will study deportment, etiquette, grooming, and cultural appreciation. Cultural appreciation is perhaps the most important aspect of gracious living. I am giving you an assignment to demonstrate to you that this is so. I want each of you to make a list of the fine and beautiful things you have in your homes. Ask your parents to explain to you what they are and what makes them valuable. I know you all live with beautiful things, which you probably take for granted. I want you to learn to appreciate them. Please bring your lists to the next class."

Jessica sighed. This sounded suspiciously like homework. Still, if it would help her get that crown, she'd do it.

Mrs. Beaumont held a book high over her head. "Lesson number one," she said. "Posture."

She placed the book on top of her head and then glided across the room with her head high, her shoulders back, and her arms swinging gracefully at her sides.

"Who would like to try it next? Mademoiselle Gilbert, how about you?"

Jessica turned to look at Patty Gilbert. She was tall and slim, with smooth coffee-colored skin and a long neck. Jessica knew that Patty was a very serious ballet student, but that was all she knew about her. Patty didn't hang around much with the other kids at school, even though she'd lived in Sweet Valley for more than a year.

Patty sighed and took the book from Mrs. Beaumont. She plopped it on top of her head and walked effortlessly across the room.

"Beautifully done," Mrs. Beaumont said, clapping. Patty rolled her eyes and returned to the group.

"That was pretty impressive," Jessica whispered.

Patty blew her breath out impatiently. "I've been able to do that since first-year ballet. I don't know why my mother is making me take this dopey course."

Probably because of your snotty personality, Jessica thought. Now she thought she knew why Patty didn't have many friends. She shrugged and returned her attention to Mrs. Beaumont.

"I hope you all will be able to do this as easily," Mrs. Beaumont was saying. "Who will be next?"

"I will," Jessica volunteered, hurrying toward Mrs. Beaumont. She knew that if she was going to win that tiara, she'd better start campaigning right away. Janet wouldn't be easy to beat.

Mrs. Beaumont placed the book on Jessica's head. "Keep your head high," she advised. "And go slowly."

It was harder than Patty had made it look. But Jessica managed to get halfway across the room before the book fell to the floor.

Janet burst out laughing, and Jessica's face flushed. "Think you can do it better?" she challenged.

Mrs. Beaumont wagged her finger at Jessica. "No, no," she admonished. "That didn't sound very polite. Manners are very important and I want us always to be aware of that. Would you like to rephrase that question in a more courteous way?"

Jessica blushed. Then she turned to Janet. "Please forgive me," she said politely. "I didn't mean to sound so rude. What I should have said is, maybe you will have more luck than I did. I truly hope so."

"Very good," Mrs. Beaumont said approvingly. "Mademoiselle Janet, perhaps you would be good enough to try."

Janet stepped forward and Jessica placed the book on her head. *I hope she trips*, Jessica thought sourly. But she gave Janet her sweetest smile. "Good luck."

As Janet straightened up and began to walk, Jessica managed to put her foot right in Janet's path. Janet fell forward and sprawled on the floor.

"Oh dear," Jessica exclaimed in her prissiest voice. "I'm so terribly sorry. I *do* apologize."

Janet picked herself up and took a step in Jessica's direction. "You did that on purpose," she said angrily.

There were some giggles from the Unicorns.

"Janet, dear," Mrs. Beaumont said, "I'm sure Jessica would never do such a thing. Please remember that I want you to act like ladies. Accept her apology and join your friends."

"Please don't give it a thought, Jessica," Janet said through tight lips. "I'm sure it was an accident."

"Very nice. All right. Now, let us see how Mademoiselle Elizabeth does," Mrs. Beaumont suggested, signaling for Elizabeth to step forward.

Elizabeth walked to the front of the room and placed the book on her head. She took one step and the book thudded to the floor.

"It looks as though I have a lot to learn," Elizabeth said.

Mrs. Beaumont smiled her polite smile. "Well, that is why you are here, yes?"

"That's right," Elizabeth answered, giving Mrs. Beaumont a level stare.

"You're getting better," Jessica commented as she watched Lila walk across the living room with the dictionary balanced on her head.

It was Saturday afternoon, and the two girls were at the Fowler mansion. Mr. Fowler was out of town on business and only the housekeeper, Mrs. Pervis, was at home with the girls.

Lila scowled. "I can't believe this stuff is really going to help me with meeting royalty, or with anything else, for that matter. If you have enough money, people don't care how you act." She tossed the dictionary onto the couch. "Here, you practice for a while. I'm going to work on my list."

Jessica picked up the book and placed it carefully on her head. She took a few steps, trying to glide the way Patty had. "Haven't you finished yet?"

Lila pulled several sheets of paper from her notebook. "I've already filled three pages and those are just the artworks. I haven't even started on the furniture," she complained. "I'm never going to finish this before we're supposed to meet Melissa at the mall. If I'd known I was going to have to write a whole big paper, I wouldn't have signed up."

Brag, brag, brag, Jessica thought grumpily. Her own list was barely a page long. The only things on it were a few pieces of old jewelry that had belonged to Mrs. Wakefield's grandmother and a couple of pieces of antique furniture.

Lila chewed thoughtfully on her pen. "You know," she said, "I guess Mrs. Beaumont was right about learning to appreciate things. I never thought very much about all this stuff before—now I realize that the things in this room alone are worth a fortune."

Jessica rolled her eyes.

The doorbell rang, and Jessica and Lila heard voices in the front hall. A minute later, Mrs. Pervis came in with Richard from the Beaumont Gallery.

"*Bonjour,*" Richard said, smiling at the girls. He was holding a large square package wrapped in brown paper. "I have here the painting that your father purchased from Monsieur Beaumont," he said.

"Dad said to hang it there, over the desk," Lila said. She pointed to a bare spot on the wall.

"Perfect," Richard said. He began to pull the paper off the painting. "This is a very valuable picture, you know."

"My father would never buy anything that wasn't," Lila said with a sniff.

Just then the telephone rang and Mrs. Pervis picked it up. "Fowler residence . . . Oh yes, Mr. Fowler, it's just arrived. Yes, Lila is here. Just a moment." Mrs. Pervis nodded to Lila. "Your father would like to speak with you."

Lila headed for the door. "I'll take it in Daddy's den," she said. Mrs. Pervis waited for Lila to pick up the extension, then she hung up the phone and left the room. Jessica settled back on the couch to watch as Richard hung the painting over the desk.

"Beautiful, isn't it?" Richard said with a smile. "It's nice when we find someone with the taste and money to truly appreciate fine works of art."

"Yes," Jessica agreed, wishing her own parents would buy something incredibly expensive and classy from the Beaumonts. Why did they always have to be so . . . well . . . *ordinary?* The Wakefields had a lovely home, but it certainly wasn't as impressive or as expensively furnished as Lila's.

When Richard finished hanging the painting, he stepped back to examine his handiwork. He nodded in satisfaction. Then he looked around the living room approvingly. He wandered from one end of the room to the other, trailing his fingers over an elaborately carved table.

"Exquisite," he said with a sigh. "Truly exquisite. This is a lovely room. One would not expect to find this in California. It reminds me of some of the beautiful homes in Europe."

Jessica was glad that Lila wasn't there to hear Richard's praise. She could just imagine her friend's smug look and superior smile.

"Oh, this is nothing," Jessica said casually. "I mean, the Fowlers have a cute little place here and all, but you should see *our* house."

"Oh, really? And who is your family?" Richard asked, looking very interested.

Jessica lifted her head a little higher. "The Wakefields. And we have lots and lots of antiques and art and things like that. Most of it came from Europe."

"How very interesting," Richard said.

"My mother is an interior designer," Jessica went on. "So she knows how to pick out the very best stuff."

Richard looked impressed. "I'm sure your home is very beautiful."

"It is," Jessica confirmed.

She watched as Richard continued to walk

slowly around the room. He picked up a small porcelain bowl and examined the mark on the bottom.

"We have *two* of those at home," Jessica told him

Richard turned and gave her a surprised look. "Really? This is museum-quality, you know."

Jessica didn't, but she nodded solemnly. "I know." She looked around the room. "We have two of those, too," she said, pointing to the elaborately carved table Richard had admired. "One on each side of the living room couch."

He raised one eyebrow, looking even more impressed. "You must have a splendid home."

"Oh, yes." Jessica smiled. "My parents have spent their whole lives collecting fine furniture. We have one of those . . . and those . . . and those." Jessica pointed to every expensive-looking thing in the room. Then her eye settled on a jeweled egg that sat in a place of honor on a shelf. "And we have a whole shelf of those," she added. "My mother collects them."

Just then, Lila came back into the room. "My father asks you to thank Mr. Beaumont and tell him he'll look forward to getting the . . . uh . . . provenance?" She stumbled over the last word.

"*Provenance* is correct," Richard said. "That's a piece of paper that proves the authenticity of a piece and tells the history of its ownership. Mr. Beaumont is getting the provenance for this painting from the auction house where it was purchased." He gave them each a small bow. "It has been a pleasure meeting you young ladies." And with a slight click of his heels, he was gone.

Lila spotted a piece of paper on the floor. "What's this?" she asked, picking it up.

Jessica blushed. "That's my list for Mrs. Beaumont."

"Not much of a list," Lila said with a smirk.

Jessica scowled. *Oh well, at least I impressed Richard,* she thought sourly.

Six

◇

"Not too much, not too little. Remember, makeup should never be extreme," Mrs. Beaumont reminded them for the tenth time.

It was Monday afternoon, and the charm school students were practicing makeup application.

This is great, Jessica thought. What could be better than a class where you learned how to put on makeup? Mrs. Beaumont had divided them into groups of three, and Jessica was working with Lila and Janet. They had given each other so many makeovers in the past that they were almost like professionals. In fact, all the Unicorns seemed to be doing a great job with the assignment.

She heard a laugh from the other side of the room. When she looked over, she saw that Amy, Elizabeth, and Maria were not doing nearly as well. Maria had painted big clown lips on the other two. And Elizabeth had obviously missed her eye completely with the mascara wand. She had black streaks all over her cheeks.

They're not taking this seriously at all, Jessica thought with a frown. *It's like they're making fun of the rest of us.*

Mrs. Beaumont tapped her on the shoulder. "May I speak to you for a moment," she whispered.

"Sure," Jessica said, scrambling out of her seat and preparing to follow Mrs. Beaumont.

Mrs. Beaumont lifted her eyebrows. "Manners," she murmured. "Let's not forget our manners."

Jessica flushed. Then she cleared her throat and made eye contact with both Lila and Janet. "Pardon me," she said politely. "Would you excuse me for just a moment?"

Janet gave Jessica her sweetest smile. "Of course, Jessica. We'd be happy to excuse you."

"Nicely done," Mrs. Beaumont said approvingly. "Both of you are doing beautifully when it comes to manners and poise. I can see that there's going to be some real competition for the title of Queen of Charm."

She took Jessica by the hand and led her out of earshot of the others. "I was a little concerned," she said. She reached into her pocket and pulled out the list that Jessica had turned in at the beginning of class. "Your list describes some valuable pieces of jewelry. I hope your mother keeps them in a bank safe-deposit box or in a safe at home."

Jessica grinned. "Nope. It's all stuffed down in the toe of an old tennis shoe in the kitchen broom closet. Mom says no burglar would ever think to look there."

Mrs. Beaumont frowned. "But surely you have an alarm system," she insisted. "To protect all the other valuable things in your home."

Jessica blinked in confusion. *Other valuable things?*

Mrs. Beaumont went on. "I am curious, Jessica, why neither you nor your sister has put them on your list. If one lives with beautiful and costly things, as you and your sister do, it is important to appreciate them."

Suddenly, Jessica realized what Mrs. Beaumont was talking about. Richard must have told her about his conversation with Jessica at Lila's house.

Jessica thought fast. "My parents don't like to make a big deal about their things," she said, trying to sound nonchalant. "They don't want to give burglars or kidnappers any ideas. They think things like alarm systems are a tip-off to crooks."

"I see," said Mrs. Beaumont quietly.

At that moment giggles erupted from the corner of the room where Elizabeth and her friends were working. Mrs. Beaumont's eyes darted in their direction. She stared for a moment at Elizabeth, who was painting bright green eye shadow all the way up to her eyebrows, then turned her gaze back on Jessica. Her mouth curved into an ingratiating smile. "You and your sister are quite different, I think. You look just alike. But inside, you are not the same. You are serious about these classes, while Elizabeth seems to take them very lightly."

There was more laughter from Elizabeth and Amy. Jessica pursed her lips in annoyance. "You're right. I don't even know why she signed up. I guess she and her friends are just trying to make fun of me and the Unicorns. They think this is dumb and that you and Mr. Beaumont are a couple of phonies."

Mrs. Beaumont lifted her eyebrows. "Is that so? Then perhaps it's time to show her that we are serious about what we do here." Mrs. Beaumont cleared her throat. "Mademoiselle Elizabeth!"

Elizabeth looked up from her makeup mirror.

"May I have everyone's attention, please?" Mrs. Beaumont said, clapping her hands.

The room fell silent. "I want you all to look at Mademoiselle Elizabeth," Mrs. Beaumont announced. She beckoned to Elizabeth to stand. "Some of you," she said, "are not taking this class as seriously as I would hope. Mademoiselle Elizabeth, you said the other day you have a lot to learn. Please do not waste your time or mine by being silly with your friends. What I am trying to teach you girls is not merely charm, but communication. What do you want to tell people about yourself?"

This is a switch, Jessica thought with satisfaction. *Usually it's Elizabeth who's getting all the praise in class and me who's getting yelled at.*

"Look at your posture," continued Mrs. Beaumont, shaking her head. "It's terrible. That slump in your spine tells people that you feel small and unimportant. Your makeup is poorly applied and sloppy. That tells people that you can't take time to do things properly. You have been laughing and talking during class, and that tells people that you are ill-mannered. Walk across the room, please, and let us see if you have worked on your carriage and bearing."

Elizabeth bit her lip and began to attempt a graceful walk. Halfway across the room, the toe of one of her tennis shoes caught the heel of the other and she tripped.

The other girls laughed, and Elizabeth blushed.

Mrs. Beaumont put her hands on her hips.

"I have been in countries far, far away where your head would be cut off if you tripped and fell in front of their queen. Be grateful, mademoiselle, that we have not yet crowned a queen who could order your execution after such a poor performance."

Elizabeth's lip trembled. Then she burst into tears, buried her face in her hands, and ran sobbing from the room.

Jessica instinctively started after her, but Mrs. Beaumont clutched her arm. "Wait," she said. "It's for her own good, remember?"

"I guess so," Jessica muttered uncertainly, staring after her sister.

As soon as she emerged into the empty hallway, Elizabeth broke into a broad grin. This was the perfect opportunity to do a little snooping.

She walked down the hall past the ladies' room. Next to the ladies' room was a pay phone, and a stairwell nearby led down to the street door. At the farthest end of the hall was an office. Beyond it was a second stairwell leading to the gallery below.

Elizabeth paused outside the office door. Painted on the frosted glass window were the words *Beaumont Charm School*. Elizabeth listened for a moment. No noise came from within, so she steathily turned the knob and walked into the office. As she entered she noticed that the room contained a large desk, a couple of chairs, and a file cabinet. Behind them, near the far wall, was a coatrack with three bulky raincoats hung in a clump. There were no other furnishings.

Elizabeth hurried over to the file cabinet. As soon as she opened one of the drawers, she spotted files with familiar names on them—Fowler, Riteman, Howell, and others. She pulled out the Riteman file and flipped through the contents. The file contained bills of sale for two pieces of furniture and a painting. Then she flipped through the Fowler file and saw the bill of sale for the painting Lila's father had bought.

So far everything looks legitimate, Elizabeth thought. *I have to find some proof that the things the Beaumonts sold are fakes*. Before she could look any further, however, she heard footsteps coming up the stairs from the gallery.

Elizabeth jammed the files back into place and shut the drawer. Suddenly the footsteps were right outside the door. There was no time to escape. Elizabeth looked quickly around the room and her eyes settled on the coatrack. Just as the door opened she dove behind the thick folds of the raincoats.

The footsteps that came into the room were

heavy and deliberate. *It must be Mr. Beaumont,* thought Elizabeth. She heard the squeaking of the swivel chair at the desk as he sat down.

Elizabeth carefully peeked out from behind the raincoats. She saw Mr. Beaumont lean forward, pick up the telephone, and dial.

There was a pause, and then he began to speak. "Hello, Hans? It's me, Beaumont . . . yeah . . . yeah . . . That's right. Fowler bought the painting. . . . No, he's not suspicious. Nobody is. . . . Why should they be? Margaret's taking care of everything. We'll continue as planned. Goodbye." He hung up the phone.

Margaret! Elizabeth sucked in her breath. Margaret—not Monique. *I was right,* Elizabeth thought. *I was right all along. Mrs. Beaumont is really Margaret Rudenthaler and she and her husband are selling phony art and antiques. The charm school is just a front for a phony business.*

Elizabeth's heart was pounding. She had stumbled onto a major criminal conspiracy. If Mr. Beaumont caught her spying on him, she could be in serious danger. *I've got to get out of here,* she thought desperately.

She peeked again around the jumble of raincoats on the coatrack. Mr. Beaumont was still at his desk, looking through a pile of papers. His back was to Elizabeth—and the open office door.

The door was only a few yards away. If she was *very* careful and *very* quiet, she could tiptoe out without being seen.

Elizabeth silently put one foot out and began to slide from behind the coatrack. Just then Mr. Beaumont swiveled his chair around to face her and she ducked back just in time.

Elizabeth held her breath. The room was so quiet, she was sure Mr. Beaumont would hear her short, rapid breaths.

She heard the chair squeak as Mr. Beaumont swiveled back around to face the desk. *Here we go again.* Elizabeth waited for a few seconds, listening carefully. She peered out and saw Mr. Beaumont's back. He was hunched over the desk. Elizabeth took a deep breath and slid from behind the rack. She tiptoed straight for the door. She had just slipped through and into the hall when she heard the chair give out another loud squeak.

That was close, Elizabeth thought, taking a deep breath. *Christine Davenport couldn't have done it better herself.*

Elizabeth hurried down the hall to the ladies' room. Since she was supposed to be sobbing her eyes out in there, she figured it might be a good idea to stop in and dab a little water on her face before heading back to class. But just as she was about to push open the door, Mrs. Beaumont came barreling out, practically knocking Elizabeth over.

Elizabeth stumbled backwards as Mrs. Beaumont glared at her. "Where have you been?" she demanded. "I've been in here twice to look for you."

"I . . . uh . . . went outside for some air," Elizabeth stammered.

Mrs. Beaumont frowned, as if she didn't quite believe her. Her eyes darted down the hall and rested for a moment on the open office door. Then she looked back at Elizabeth.

Elizabeth forced herself to look Mrs. Beaumont in the eye.

"Go back to class, please," Mrs. Beaumont snapped.

As Elizabeth walked down the hall toward the studio, she could feel Mrs. Beaumont's eyes watching her the whole way.

Seven

"I don't believe it!" Amy exclaimed.

"You're *sure* you heard him call her Margaret?" Maria asked for about the tenth time.

Elizabeth nodded vigorously. "Do you guys think I would make up something like this?"

The three girls had just gotten out of charm school, and Elizabeth had just finished telling Amy and Maria about what she'd overheard in the Beaumonts' office.

It had taken every bit of her patience to wait until they were safely out of the building to spill the story. As soon as they were a block away, Elizabeth had hopped off her bicycle and signaled for her friends to do the same. Now the three of them sat on a bench in front of a little park that had been created out of an empty lot.

"No, I don't think you're making it up," Amy said thoughtfully, "but I do know that you've been reading an awful lot of Amanda Howard mysteries recently—maybe your imagination is going a little crazy."

"I'm not imagining this," Elizabeth retorted. "I heard it exactly the way I told you."

Amy looked thoughtful and was silent for a moment. "I believe you," she said finally.

"I believe you, too," Maria said solemnly. "At first it was like a game. I was just sort of *pretending* we were solving a mystery. But now . . . this is serious. Do you think we ought to call the police?"

"And tell them what?" Amy demanded. "That Elizabeth was eavesdropping from behind a bunch of raincoats and overheard a conversation? That's not much for the police to go on."

"Amy's right," Elizabeth agreed. "Christine Davenport would never bring in the police at this stage."

"So what would she do?" Maria asked.

Elizabeth had been asking herself that same question. "We'll have to break this case on our own."

"But how?" Amy wondered.

"By getting the proof. And I think I know where to look."

"Shh," warned Maria. "Here comes company."

Elizabeth and Amy looked over and saw Jessica, Lila, and Janet approaching.

"Feeling better?" Janet asked Elizabeth in a phony sweet voice.

"What?" asked Elizabeth. Then she remembered that she was supposed to be upset. "Oh! Yes, I'm feeling better. I'm just going to have to try harder."

"I must say, Elizabeth, I'm a little surprised to see you getting into trouble for goofing around," Janet said condescendingly. "I thought you were supposed to be Little Miss Perfect."

Amy was quick to jump to Elizabeth's defense. "She could ace this stuff with her eyes closed if she wanted," Amy said hotly. "In fact, I wouldn't be surprised if she ended up winning the Mademoiselle Manners Award."

"Hah!" Janet said. "Don't make me laugh. That award is going to be won by a Unicorn. And we all know which one. Right, Jessica?"

Jessica gave Janet a dirty look. "Well, if you mean me, you're right. I hope you're practicing your curtsy."

Janet smiled sweetly. "I think that might be a little premature. What do you think, Lila?"

Lila bit her lip in confusion. Elizabeth had to stifle a giggle. She could see that Lila was debating with herself over whose side to take. Jessica was

Lila's best friend, but Janet was president of the Unicorns and Lila's cousin.

Lila looked at her watch. "Oh my, look at the time. I'd better get home," she said, hurrying off.

"Chicken," muttered Amy under her breath Elizabeth and Maria began to giggle.

On Wednesday afternoon after charm class, Elizabeth, Amy, and Maria went into the ladies' room, locked themselves in one of the stalls, and waited. In the hall outside, they could hear the laughter and footsteps of the other girls as they left.

After the last set of footsteps had died away, Amy glanced at Elizabeth. Elizabeth shook her head and mouthed, "Wait." There wasn't a sound to be heard except the dripping of a faucet in one of the sinks. The girls waited silently for what seemed like an eternity.

Amy sighed and shifted to a more comfortable position. "I didn't realize detective work was so boring," she whispered.

"Shh," Elizabeth cautioned. "We've got to stay in here until the floor is empty. I have to get into those files again. I just know the proof we need is there."

Maria pulled a paperback from her purse and settled down to wait. Amy began to doodle on a notepad. Elizabeth checked the batteries in the flashlight she had brought with her.

Finally, they heard a solitary pair of footsteps walk down the hall and into the stairwell just outside the ladies' room. They heard a loud click as the person threw the main light switch, leaving the ladies' room in darkness. Then they heard the footsteps move down the stairs and fade away out of hearing.

Elizabeth waited a few more minutes just to be on the safe side. Then she turned on her flashlight and tiptoed out of the stall. "Let's go," she said quietly.

The three girls slipped out of the ladies' room and walked down the hall toward the office. Elizabeth put her hand on the knob. It turned easily, and the door opened with a slight creak.

"If the Beaumonts are big criminal masterminds," Amy whispered, "why aren't they smart enough to lock the door?"

"They probably don't think anybody is suspicious," Elizabeth answered quietly. She went over to the file cabinet.

Maria and Amy looked over Elizabeth's shoulder as she pulled several files from the drawer and spread them out. "Fowler . . . Howell . . . Riteman . . . Haver," Elizabeth muttered.

Then she gasped. There was a new file, labeled Wakefield.

Elizabeth opened the file and saw bills of sale for several expensive items. They all had been shipped to Mrs. Montgomery, one of her mother's biggest clients. "Oh, no," she said. "If Mom gets caught selling phony art and antiques, it will ruin her reputation."

Maria picked up one of the bills of sale and examined it closely. Attached to it was an official-looking piece of paper. "Look," she whispered. "It's a provenance. That's the paper that proves that what you bought is the real thing. See, it shows that a museum sold this piece to a gallery in Paris. And the gallery in Paris sold it to an auction house in New York. And the auction house in New York sold it to the Beaumonts."

Amy picked up the Howell file and flipped through it. "There's one attached to every bill of sale. Wow! The Howells have bought some really expensive stuff."

Elizabeth grabbed the Fowler file out of the drawer and began to rifle through it. "There must be something here that proves the stuff is phony. There *must* be. I'm almost sure that painting they sold Mr. Fowler is a fake." She pulled an official-looking letter out of the file and skimmed it. Her face fell. " 'Dear Mr. Fowler,' " she read slowly. " 'We apologize for the delay in sending the enclosed provenance for the Holtzinger . . .' "

"We get the picture," Maria said. "I hate to say it, but it looks as though everything is on the up and up."

"Somebody's coming!" Amy whispered suddenly. "Let's get out of here."

Amy and Maria began stuffing files back into the cabinet. "Just a minute," Elizabeth protested. "Just give me a few more seconds. I know the proof is here somewhere."

But already the girls could hear the sound of footsteps coming up the stairs from the gallery below. The sound was faint, but getting louder.

"Let's *go*," Amy insisted as she and Maria darted out the door.

Elizabeth took one last look at the Fowler file. Then she shoved it back into place and raced out the door . . . where she bumped right into Mr. Beaumont!

Mr. Beaumont looked stunned. "What are you doing in my office?" he demanded angrily.

Elizabeth stared at him, trembling from head to toe.

"What are you doing here?" Mr. Beaumont repeated.

"I was . . . I was . . . I was . . ." Elizabeth looked up and down the hall for Amy and Maria.

Mr. Beaumont's face was pale with anger.

"Elizabeth!" she heard a cheerful voice call.

Mr. Beaumont started. Elizabeth looked up and saw Amy and Maria stepping out of the ladies' room. Amy held up her backpack. "I found your backpack," she called out with a giggle.

"I—I was looking for my backpack," Elizabeth stammered to Mr. Beaumont, silently congratulating Amy on her quick thinking.

"In my office?" he asked skeptically.

Elizabeth swallowed. "I thought maybe somebody had found it and put it in there," she explained. "But I must have left it in the ladies' room."

Mr. Beaumont shook his head and turned away.

"Good night," Elizabeth called to him as she hurried down the hall to join Amy and Maria.

The three of them bolted down the stairs and out of the building. When they were safely outside, Elizabeth let out her breath with a long sigh. "Way to go, you guys," she said. "Amanda Howard would be proud of you."

Amy shook her head. "That was close, Elizabeth. We could get into really serious trouble.

What if he calls our parents and tells them he caught you snooping in his office?"

"What could he say?" Elizabeth said. "'I'm upset that your daughter was about to prove we're in the phony art and antiques business'?"

Amy and Maria exchanged glances. "Elizabeth," Maria said patiently, "we weren't about to find any proof. There's no proof to find. You saw the papers. Let's face it—we can't be detectives if there's no mystery to solve."

Elizabeth felt so frustrated, she thought she might cry. "But didn't you see how angry Mr. Beaumont looked?" she asked.

"Sure," Maria said. "Who wouldn't be angry if they caught some kid snooping around their office?"

"I'm right," Elizabeth said firmly. "I just know I'm right." She shook her head. "And it's more important than ever that we get to the bottom of it. My mom's career may be at stake."

That evening, Elizabeth worried all through dinner. She knew how much her mother loved being an interior designer. If anybody ever found out she had bought a bunch of phony stuff for a client, she'd be ruined.

I've got to say something to her, Elizabeth

thought. *If I don't and the story comes out, I'll feel terrible.*

So after dinner, Elizabeth went into the kitchen and confided all her suspicions to Mrs. Wakefield, leaving out the parts about sneaking into Mr. Beaumont's office, eavesdropping on his phone conversation, and looking through his files.

"Honestly, Elizabeth," Mrs. Wakefield said when Elizabeth had finished. "It isn't like you to jump to conclusions about perfectly nice, respectable people."

"But I know I'm right," Elizabeth insisted. "The Beaumonts are up to no good."

Jessica came into the kitchen just in time to hear Elizabeth's last sentence. "She's just trying to get out of going back to charm school," Jessica said. "She and her friends have been goofing around and acting silly and Mrs. Beaumont really let her have it today."

"Is that true, Elizabeth?" Mrs. Wakefield asked.

"Yes, but—"

Mrs. Wakefield didn't let her finish. "Please, Elizabeth. I'm surprised at you. Your father and I are paying good money for you to take this class. So I'd like you to get serious about it and stop imagining that the Beaumonts are spies."

"Crooks," Elizabeth corrected.

"She's just jealous," Jessica said. "Because for once, I'm better at something than she is."

Elizabeth signed and trudged out of the kitchen. *What would Christine Davenport do now?* she wondered.

Elizabeth woke the next morning with an idea. She got dressed quickly, gulped down her breakfast, and arrived at school a half-hour early.

Mr. Sweeney, the art teacher, was almost always in the art studio before classes started. He liked to have the time to work on his own paintings.

Elizabeth paused in the door of the art studio, watching him paint with broad, bold strokes. *Should I really do this?* she asked herself. Then a little voice in her head answered, *Christine Davenport would.*

"Mr. Sweeney?" Elizabeth said.

Mr. Sweeney looked up and gave her a pleased smile. "Elizabeth! What are you doing here so early?"

Elizabeth took a deep breath. "You told the class you had a friend who was a curator at the museum," she said. "Would he know how to authenticate a painting?"

Eight

◇

"Have I *ever* been wrong?" Elizabeth asked.

"Not as long as I've known you," Maria said. "But then again, I haven't known you that long."

"Do I *look* like a nut?" Elizabeth asked.

"Well, not really," Amy admitted.

"Then why are you two backing out on me?" Elizabeth demanded. "Are you detectives or aren't you?"

The three girls were in the Wakefields' kitchen debating their next move over a plate of chocolate chip cookies.

Maria took a sip of milk and smiled. "I guess getting caught by Mr. Beaumont spooked us," she said. "We're letting ourselves be intimidated. So—I'll do it."

"Way to go," Elizabeth said. She turned to Amy. "What about you? Are you in or out?"

Amy frowned. "All right, I guess I'm in. But if it were anybody but Elizabeth Wakefield trying to talk me into this, I'd run in the other direction."

"Great," Elizabeth said, going to the telephone. "You're sure you can sound like my mom?"

"Well, of course," said Maria, perfectly imitating Mrs. Wakefield's voice. "I'm surprised you would doubt me, Elizabeth."

"That's great, Maria," Elizabeth said, laughing.

Maria grinned and dialed the Beaumont Gallery. "Mr. Beaumont? Hello, this is Alice Wakefield. . . . Fine. How are you? . . . How nice. The reason I'm calling, Mr. Beaumont, is that I wanted to ask if you could arrange to meet me on Saturday afternoon at the Fowler home. Mr. Fowler has hired me to redecorate his living room, and I was hoping you could advise me on some pieces of furniture and art you think would be suitable. . . . Yes. One o'clock will be fine. Thank you. Goodbye."

Maria hung up the phone and giggled. "He'll be there. Now for Mr. Fowler."

Elizabeth handed Maria the phone book, and Maria dialed Lila's father's office number. She again gave her name as Alice Wakefield and then waited while Mr. Fowler's secretary transferred the call. "Mr. Fowler?" Maria asked in Mrs. Wakefield's voice. "Just fine, thank you. I was wondering if I could come by your house on Saturday afternoon. I'm doing some research on antiques for the, uh . . ." Maria looked flustered and waved frantically to Elizabeth.

"Designers' Association," Elizabeth hissed.

"Designers' Association," Maria said, barely missing a beat. "I'd like to look at some of your things and ask you some questions. . . . Excuse me? . . . Oh, yes. How does one o'clock sound? . . . Wonderful. I'll see you then. Goodbye."

Maria hung up the phone and the three girls burst into laughter.

"Now all you have to do is call my mom tonight, pretend to be Mrs. Beaumont, and ask her to meet you at the Fowlers' for some design advice." Elizabeth reached for another cookie. "I'm going to crack this case once and for all."

On Saturday afternoon, Elizabeth, Amy, and Maria watched the Fowlers' front door from behind a hedge in the sweeping front lawn. Mr. Beaumont had already arrived, and Mrs. Wakefield had just gone up the walk and been admitted by Mrs. Pervis.

"Now," Elizabeth said, glancing at her friends.

The three girls hurried up to the front door and rang the bell. Mrs. Pervis opened the door, and as soon as Elizabeth stepped into the foyer, she heard the sound of several confused voices talking at once in the living room.

Elizabeth stepped into the room and saw that Jessica and Lila were there, too, watching as Mr. Fowler, Mrs. Wakefield, and Mr. Beaumont tried to figure out what was going on.

"Excuse me!" Elizabeth said loudly. "I think I may be able to clear up the confusion."

The grownups looked up in surprise, and Jessica and Lila exchanged a curious look. "This should be good," Lila muttered, just loudly enough for Elizabeth to overhear.

"Elizabeth!" Mrs. Wakefield exclaimed. "What are you doing here?"

This is going to be harder than I thought, Elizabeth thought as five pairs of eyes stared at her expectantly. "I guess you're all wondering why you're gathered here. We arranged it. I mean, Amy and Maria and I." She gestured behind her, and her friends stepped forward shyly.

"What on earth?" Mrs. Wakefield began.

"Maria disguised her voice," Elizabeth explained. "She called Mr. Beaumont and Mr. Fowler and pretended to be you. And then she called you, Mom, and pretended to be Mrs. Beaumont."

Mr. Beaumont narrowed his eyes. "Is this some kind of a joke?" he asked grimly.

"It's not a joke," Elizabeth said quickly. "I just needed to get you all here together. But there's still one person missing. And when he gets here . . ." Elizabeth faltered. *Act like a real detective,* she told herself sternly. She drew herself up to her full height. "When he gets here," she said again, "I intend to prove that that man"—she pointed to Mr. Beaumont—"is a crook. And that painting"—she pointed to the painting over the desk—"is a fake!"

Behind her, Elizabeth heard Amy and Maria gasp. They probably hadn't expected her to be quite so dramatic.

There was a stunned silence. Then Jessica and Lila broke into giggles.

Mr. Beaumont had turned pale, and his mouth was set in a narrow line. Mrs. Wakefield stared at Elizabeth as if she thought her daughter had lost her mind. And the corner of Mr. Fowler's mouth twitched, as though he was trying not to laugh. "Elizabeth," he began, "I can assure you that I am perfectly satisfied with the authenticity of the painting. There's really no need—"

Just then, the doorbell rang.

"That's him," Elizabeth said.

"Who?" Mrs. Wakefield demanded.

"Mr. Kolker, a curator at the museum," Elizabeth answered.

Mrs. Wakefield put her hand over her forehead, as if she had suddenly developed a terrible headache. "I see," she said.

A moment later Mrs. Pervis showed in a neatly dressed man with a short brown beard. "How do you do?" the man said politely. "I'm John Kolker from the Sweet Valley Museum. Mrs. Wakefield invited me here to authenticate a painting."

Mrs. Wakefield shot a threatening look in Elizabeth's direction. "I'm Mrs. Wakefield," she said. "But I'm afraid you were brought here under false—"

"*Mom!*" Elizabeth interrupted. "Please! I know what I'm doing." Elizabeth turned to Mr. Kolker. "Can you tell a real Holtzinger from a fake one?" she asked eagerly.

"Oh, yes." Mr. Kolker smiled. "They're quite rare and unmistakable." His eyes searched the room and stopped when they saw the painting over the desk. "That's the painting in question, I assume."

"That's right," Elizabeth said.

Mr. Kolker put on his glasses and stepped over to the painting. He peered intently at the canvas.

Elizabeth bit her lip nervously. Everyone's eyes were glued to Mr. Kolker. He moved even closer, inspecting every inch of the canvas.

He's going to say it's a fake, Elizabeth thought expectantly. *Then everybody will see that I was right all along. Maybe Mr. Fowler will be so grateful that he really will hire Mom to redecorate his house.*

Mr. Kolker removed his glasses and polished them with his handkerchief. He cleared his throat and turned to face the group. Elizabeth held her breath. "There's no doubt about it," Mr. Kolker said. "This painting is a genuine Holtzinger."

The room was so quiet that Elizabeth would swear she could hear the blood rush to her face. She had never felt so embarrassed in her whole life. *I wish the floor would just open up so I could fall through it,* she thought.

Finally, Mr. Kolker broke the silence. He pointed to the painting. "See the way the light appears to emanate from the background? It's impossible to imitate. Simply impossible. Others have tried. But no one's ever been able to duplicate the results."

No one else said a word for another minute.

Elizabeth glanced at Amy and Maria. Both of them stared intently at their feet, refusing to meet her eyes. Both of their faces were bright red.

Suddenly, Jessica and Lila burst into laughter.

Mr. Fowler recovered his wits first. "I'm so sorry to have wasted your time," he said to Mr. Kolker.

"Not at all," Mr. Kolker replied. "Seeing a Holtzinger is a rare pleasure."

"Why don't you step into the other room?" Mr. Fowler said, gesturing to a door on the far side of the living room. "I have some other paintings in there that you might like to see. I'll join you in a moment."

"Thank you," Mr. Kolker said with a smile. He exited through the door Mr. Fowler had indicated.

Elizabeth stole a look at her mother's face. It was white with anger and embarrassment. Mrs. Wakefield turned to Mr. Beaumont and offered her hand. "I'm so terribly sorry," she said. "My husband and I will have a serious talk with Elizabeth tonight. I'm sure Amy and Maria's parents will have a few choice words to say to them as well."

Mr. Beaumont still looked angry. He glared at Elizabeth and Amy and Maria. But then he forced his lips into a wry smile. "Do not give it a thought," he said graciously, taking Mrs. Wakefield's hand. "It is the television. Perhaps they watch it too much. It gives them strange ideas. Anyway, it was a pleasure to see you again, and also to visit Mr. Fowler's lovely home."

Jessica and Lila were still laughing hysterically.

"Jessica," Mrs. Wakefield said. "Stop that right now!"

Jessica and Lila quieted down immediately. Jessica hiccuped. "Hey, don't yell at me. I didn't do anything." She looked at Lila and giggled. Soon, they were both shrieking with laughter again.

"Why don't you girls go up to Lila's room?" Mr. Fowler suggested. He still looked as if he was trying not to laugh himself.

Lila and Jessica ran from the room, and Elizabeth could still hear their laughter as they ran up the stairs.

Mr. Fowler looked at Elizabeth and chuckled. "Elizabeth, I'm gratified to know that you and your friends are looking after my interests. But in the future, I'd appreciate it if you'd just let me know what's on your mind and dispense with the cloak-and-dagger routine." He turned to Mr. Beaumont. "Why don't I order up some coffee? Then we can sit down with Kolker and have a spirited discussion on art."

Mr. Beaumont gave them all another forced smile. "Thank you, but I am very busy." He looked at Elizabeth. "If Mademoiselle Elizabeth has no further questions," he said, "I will get back to my gallery." He turned on his heel and strode out of the room.

"I just can't believe you would do something like this," Mrs. Wakefield said.

It was an hour later, and Elizabeth and her mother were in the car on the way home. They already had dropped off Maria and Amy. Mrs. Wakefield had gone inside both girls' houses and filled their parents in on what had happened.

Neither Amy nor Maria had said one word to Elizabeth after they left the Fowlers'. Elizabeth wondered if they would ever speak to her again.

"How could you do something so childish— so *dishonest?* Asking Maria to call busy people and pretend to be someone else, accusing Mr. Beaumont of being a crook, wasting everybody's time like that. What were you thinking?"

A tear began to roll down Elizabeth's cheek. How could she have been so wrong? How could she have done such terrible things? And how could she have dragged her friends into it?

"I want you to send a written apology to every single person involved—*tonight!*" Mrs. Wakefield said. "And you're grounded. No phone calls, no TV, no horseback riding, no trips to the mall. The only place you're going is to school . . . oh yes, and charm class."

"Mom!" Elizabeth protested. "I can't go back there now."

"Oh, yes you can. And you will. That's part of your punishment. You're going to attend those classes, and you're going to pay attention. I think your behavior today proved that you have a lot to learn about good manners."

Elizabeth hung her head.

"Oh, and one more thing—*no more Amanda Howard mysteries for a year!*"

Nine

"Hey, Detective Wakefield!" a voice shouted from the other end of the hall. "I can't find my algebra book. Think you can figure out who stole it?" Laughter broke out all around.

Elizabeth didn't bother to look. She recognized Bruce Patman's voice. It was only nine in the morning and already the story was all over school. *Lila and Jessica sure have been busy,* she thought unhappily.

Elizabeth hurried to her math class. When she sat down at her desk, she saw that somebody had left a magnifying glass on it. She heard snickering from the desks behind her and felt her face flush.

Maria came in just before the bell and took her seat. Elizabeth tried to catch her eye, but Maria refused to look at her.

"Hey, I hear there's going to be a new detective series on TV next season," Dennis Cookman called out. "It's called *The Elizabeth Wakefield Mystery Hour.*"

"Oh, yeah?" Ellen Riteman asked with a laugh.

"Yeah!" Dennis said. "Maria Slater is playing the role of Elizabeth Wakefield, and Amy Sutton is writing the scripts." Dennis smirked. "It's a whole new concept in detective shows. The twist is that there's never actually any mystery to start with."

"Maybe they should call it *The Elizabeth Wakefield Paranoia Hour,*" Ellen suggested. Everybody in the class began to laugh.

Elizabeth couldn't stand it anymore. "Shut up," she said irritably.

"Oooooooohhhh," Dennis said. "That didn't sound very charming to me. Maybe you'd better quit looking for mysteries at that charm school and start learning better manners."

Smack! Elizabeth jumped as a wad of paper bounced off Dennis's head.

"Hey!" he cried out in surprise.

Elizabeth blinked. The wad of paper had come from Maria's direction.

"Lay off," Maria ordered.

Before Dennis could respond, Ms. Wyler came in and called the class to order.

*   *   *

"Thanks for sticking up for me," Elizabeth said as she caught up with Maria after class.

Maria gave her a tight smile. "You don't deserve it after what you got us into. But like it or not, we're going to have to stick together. We're in for some pretty rough teasing."

"Elizabeth! Elizabeth! Come quickly!" Janet Howell called out in a panicky voice. She stood in the hall outside a classroom door, gesturing frantically. "Come here. We need you."

Elizabeth and Maria ran toward Janet, whose face was pale with fright. "What is it?" Elizabeth asked in alarm.

Janet covered her face with her hands. "It's horrible. Just horrible. Look."

Elizabeth and Maria peeked cautiously into the classroom. Bruce Patman lay on the floor with a rubber knife clutched between his armpit and rib cage. He had smeared red paint on his shirt to look like blood. His eyes were closed and his tongue was hanging out of his mouth.

Laughter erupted behind them. Elizabeth turned and saw that about a dozen kids were gathered for the joke, including several of the Unicorns.

"Who did it, Elizabeth?" Janet asked in a loud stage whisper. "Can you think of a suspect to accuse?"

Elizabeth rolled her eyes. "Considering that the victim is Bruce Patman, I'd say the murderer could have been anybody who got the chance. And if I find the killer, I'm going to buy him or her an ice cream soda."

Everyone laughed again. Mandy Miller clapped Elizabeth on the back. "Good comeback," she said with a grin.

Elizabeth and Maria pushed through the crowd and worked their way back to their lockers. "That's the way to play it," Maria said approvingly. "Just pretend you think it's as funny as they do. Pretty soon they'll get bored and forget it ever happened."

Elizabeth sighed. "I hope you're right."

At lunchtime, Elizabeth spotted Amy and Maria sitting by themselves at a table in a corner of the cafeteria. She took her tray over to join them. Amy gave her a long look and didn't smile. "I'm grounded," she said. "Forever."

"Me, too," Maria added.

"Me, three," Elizabeth said. "It's my fault and I'm sorry."

Amy shook her head. "You wouldn't believe what I've been through this morning."

"Oh, yes we would," Maria said. "We've been going through it, too."

"Way to go, Wakefield," Amy said grimly. "There's only one thing to be grateful for—at least we didn't turn the Beaumonts in to the police. Then we'd look like even bigger fools."

Elizabeth's face burned. The worst part of this whole situation was having Amy angry at her. After Jessica, Amy was her oldest and best friend in the world. "I'm sorry," Elizabeth blurted out, close to tears. "I'm sorry I got you into trouble. I'm sorry people are teasing you. And I'm sorry I ever *mentioned* Amanda Howard. But I heard what I heard. And I still think I'm right!"

"Elizabeth!" Maria and Amy said together.

"I can't help it," Elizabeth said stubbornly. "I still think there's something fishy about the Beaumont Gallery—even if I can't prove it."

Amy tried to keep a stern expression on her face. But when she saw the tears welling up in Elizabeth's eyes, she relented. She put her arm around Elizabeth's shoulders and gave her a smile. "Look, it's OK. Suspect whomever you want of whatever you want. Just promise us that from now on, you'll leave us out of it, and we'll all be friends again. Right, Maria?"

Maria laughed and nodded.

Elizabeth smiled reluctantly. "It's a deal."

* * *

"Very good, Elizabeth," Mrs. Beaumont said.

The first portion of Monday's charm school class was devoted to cultural appreciation. Mrs. Beaumont had turned out the lights and was showing slides of famous paintings. Elizabeth had just correctly identified the first three paintings.

It had taken all of Elizabeth's courage to walk into class that afternoon. She had been afraid Mrs. Beaumont would yell at her, but so far she hadn't said a word about Saturday's incident.

"Elizabeth," Mrs. Beaumont said sweetly, "you are doing so well identifying paintings. Let's try one more. Tell me what this one is, please."

Mrs. Beaumont advanced the projector and the class broke into laughter. It was a slide of the Holtzinger painting Mr. Fowler had bought.

Elizabeth gritted her teeth. "It's a Holtzinger," she said. "Or a very good imitation of one," she added under her breath.

Amy elbowed her in the ribs. "Cool it," she whispered.

"Very good, Mademoiselle Elizabeth," Mrs. Beaumont said. "Let us move on to furniture. Mademoiselle Janet, can you please tell us the difference between a sideboard and a hunt board?"

* * *

"Can you believe that?" Elizabeth said angrily when the girls were sent to their makeup mirrors.

"Sure I can," Amy said. "What did you expect? That she was going to shake your hand and thank you for accusing her and her husband of being crooks?"

"Shh," Maria warned. "Here she comes."

Mrs. Beaumont walked over to join the girls. She put one hand on Elizabeth's shoulder. "I wanted to thank you for your beautifully written letter of apology. And I want the three of you to know that my husband and I have no hard feelings. You all act so grown-up sometimes, we forget that you are just little girls with overactive imaginations." She gave Elizabeth a condescending pat on the head and walked away.

"Little girls!" Elizabeth hissed angrily.

"Well, that's how we acted," Maria replied. "Now let's get serious about this stuff. My parents told me that if I don't graduate from charm school with honors, I'll be grounded until I go to college."

Elizabeth sighed. Her parents had told her pretty much the same thing. Remembering the stern look on her father's face, she reached for the eye shadow.

"Everybody at school thinks Elizabeth is the biggest idiot in Sweet Valley," Janet said to Jessica and Lila as they sat at their makeup mirror. "And they think Amy and Maria are the second- and third-biggest idiots."

Jessica narrowed her eyes. She wished Janet would shut up. At first she had been glad that Elizabeth had gotten into trouble instead of her for once, but enough was enough. She was sick of hearing people like Janet make fun of her sister.

Janet smirked. "I just wish I could have been at your house on Saturday, Lila. It sounded incredibly funny."

"You're right. It was hysterical," Lila replied, leaning forward to examine the eyeliner she had just applied. "You should have seen Elizabeth's face when Mr. Kolker said that Daddy's painting was the real thing."

"How does it feel to have a sister who's a laughingstock, Jessica?" Janet teased.

Jessica looked down at the lipstick in her hand. All it would take was one little slip of the arm, and she could leave a long red mark on Janet's white blouse.

"Oops!" Jessica cried as her elbow slid across the table.

"Oh!" shrieked Janet as the lipstick left a bright red streak down her sleeve. "Look what you've done to my blouse!"

Before Jessica could say a word, Mrs. Beaumont appeared beside her. "Are we having trouble here, girls?"

Janet and Jessica glared at each other for a moment. Then Jessica remembered how much she wanted to win the Mademoiselle Manners Award. She put on an apologetic smile. "I'm so dreadfully sorry, Janet. I insist on paying to have it dry-cleaned."

Janet gritted her teeth, but then she forced a smile onto her face as well. "No, no, Jessica, my dear. Don't worry about a thing. It's machine washable."

Lila grinned at Mrs. Beaumont. "See? No problems here. We're all as charming as can be."

"Good," Mrs. Beaumont said. Then she moved to the center of the room and clapped her hands for attention. "I just wanted to remind all of you about the arrangements for Wednesday," she announced. "As you know, it's our last class. We will learn how to behave when we are introduced to royalty, and then you will be dismissed early so that you can go home and change for the party that evening. Invitations have been sent, and I have spent all morning on the phone with your families. I'm happy to report that almost all of your parents and brothers and sisters will be attending."

"Is it going to be a fancy party?" Kimberly Haver asked eagerly.

"Of course," Mrs. Beaumont said with a laugh. "The caterers are going to set up banquet tables with beautiful centerpieces. Just before dinner, I will announce the winner of the Mademoiselle Manners Award. Then our Queen of Charm will lead the class into the banquet in a procession. At the very end, each girl will come up to the front and curtsy to the Queen. Needless to say, I expect you all to demonstrate impeccable manners and poise." She smiled at the girls. "That is all for today. You are dismissed."

Jessica raised her hand. "Mrs. Beaumont, couldn't you just give us a hint about who's going to win?"

"Just a tiny hint," Janet added.

"Oh, no," Mrs. Beaumont exclaimed with a laugh. "That wouldn't be fair." But just before she walked away, she winked at Jessica.

"See that?" Jessica whispered triumphantly to Janet. "It's going to be me."

Janet glared. "Not if I have anything to say about it."

"Well, you don't." Jessica gave Janet a smug smile. "You might want to watch the way I cross the room," she said. "Your walk still looks a little clumsy to me. You wouldn't want to trip when you come to the front of the room to curtsy to me."

"You mean like this?" Janet whispered. She stuck her foot right in Jessica's path.

"Yikes!" Jessica tripped over Janet's foot and fell to the floor.

Mrs. Beaumont looked over at them. "Tsk, tsk, Mademoiselle Jessica. Watch where you step."

Jessica looked up and saw Janet grinning down at her. "Here, let me help you up—Mademoiselle Clumsy!" Janet whispered. Janet held her hand out to Jessica and helped Jessica to her feet.

"Very funny," Jessica said, giving Janet a shove.

Janet stumbled backwards and bumped into Lila. "Watch it," Lila complained.

"Shut up, Lila," Janet snapped. Then she turned back toward Jessica. "That wasn't very nice—Mademoiselle Clumsy," she hissed. Then she shoved Jessica back.

Jessica reached over and shoved Janet even harder. "Quit calling me Mademoiselle Clumsy," she ordered loudly.

Janet shoved Jessica's shoulder as hard as she could. "Make me," she challenged.

Jessica reached out to shove Janet again. But

the next thing she knew, Mrs. Beaumont was pushing them apart. "Girls! Girls! What is the meaning of this?" she exclaimed angrily.

Janet and Jessica glared at each other. "She started it," Jessica cried.

"Did not!" Janet retorted.

"Did too."

Mrs. Beaumont clapped her hands loudly. "Stop this immediately! Have you learned *nothing* in my class?"

Jessica's heart sank. Now she'd really blown her chance to be the Queen of Charm. But then she had an idea. Maybe an elaborate apology would undo the damage.

"I apologize," she said contritely. "First of all, I apologize to you, Mrs. Beaumont. My behavior was unforgivable. Please pardon me. And Janet, please forgive me for my childish outburst. It was my fault completely and I apologize."

Janet caught on immediately. Not to be outdone, she launched into her own apology. "No, no, Jessica. It was *my* fault. I apologize to you, and to Mrs. Beaumont. And also to you, Lila. I'm sure I sounded very rude. In fact, I apologize to everyone in the room."

Mrs. Beaumont gave the girls a satisfied smile. "Very nice," she said approvingly. "I think

I might be able to overlook this unfortunate incident if you both promise it will never happen again."

"I promise," Jessica said solemnly

"So do I." Janet gave Mrs. Beaumont an angelic smile.

Mrs. Beaumont nodded. Then she turned and walked away.

"I'm still going to win," Jessica whispered under her breath.

"Hah!" Janet retorted quietly.

They both stuck out their tongues.

We're sure learning a lot in charm school, Jessica thought with a little smile.

Ten

"No! No!" Mrs. Beaumont cried impatiently. *"Never* speak to a royal personage before you are spoken to. And keep your back straight when you curtsy. Try it again, Amy."

It was Wednesday afternoon, and the charm school students were gathered for their last class. Mrs. Beaumont was pretending to be a queen and the girls were taking turns being presented to her.

"Somehow, I can't believe we're ever going to need to know this stuff," Elizabeth whispered to Maria.

"Speak for yourself," Maria whispered back with a grin. "I may wind up giving a command performance at Buckingham Palace someday."

Elizabeth smiled. "Well, la-di-da for you."

"Be quiet!" Mrs. Beaumont commanded them sharply.

Elizabeth shut her mouth quickly. *Yes, Your Royal Crookedness,* she thought.

The studio door opened and several workmen came in carrying long folding tables. They leaned them against the wall and left the room again, returning a few minutes later with stacks of folding chairs.

"That will do." Mrs. Beaumont nodded at Kimberly, who had just finished curtsying. "Girls," she announced, "I'm going to let you go early today, because I know you all need time to get home and dress for the graduation banquet this evening. We also need some time to set up these tables and turn this room into a hall worthy of the Queen of Charm." She smiled. "I'll expect you back here with your families at six-thirty."

"My mother is bringing Mrs. Beaumont some flowers to apologize for my behavior," Amy whispered to Elizabeth and Maria.

"Mine, too," Maria whispered back.

"Let's be sure to enjoy ourselves at the banquet," Amy said. "Because after tonight, we probably won't get to go anywhere for a long time."

Elizabeth groaned. She felt guilty enough as it was. "I *said* I was sorry!" she said, forgetting to keep her voice down.

"I said be quiet, Elizabeth!" Mrs. Beaumont scolded. "Please pay attention. I'm trying to give you your instructions for this evening."

"Sorry," Elizabeth muttered.

"When you arrive, direct your families into this room," Mrs. Beaumont continued. "Then I want all of you to gather in the office at the end of the hall. I will announce the winner of the Mademoiselle Manners Award to you then. The Queen of Charm will wear the tiara into the dining room and lead you all in a procession around the room."

"Oh, brother," Elizabeth said.

"Shh," hissed Amy.

"After dinner, before the dessert is served, I will ask the Queen of Charm to make a short speech about what she has learned in this class and how she hopes it will change her life. After that, I want you all to approach the Queen, one at a time, and make your curtsy."

"I'm going to be sick," Elizabeth grumbled.

Maria gave her a warning look.

"That is all," Mrs. Beaumont said. "I look forward to seeing you this evening."

Elizabeth grabbed her backpack and followed Amy and Maria down the stairs and out of the building.

"Boy, Mrs. Beaumont sure was cranky today," Elizabeth commented.

"I guess she's nervous about tonight. If we really goof up or spill soup on ourselves or something, we'll make her look bad," Maria said with a laugh.

Amy stopped in front of the gallery's front window. "Look, the lights are all off. I wonder why it's closed."

"Mr. Beaumont probably has to help her get ready for the banquet," Maria said.

Elizabeth pressed her face against the window. "It looks almost empty in there."

"They've probably sold most of their stuff," Amy said.

Maria laughed. "Yeah, most of it to Janet Howell's parents."

"But wouldn't you think they'd restock?" Elizabeth asked.

Amy shrugged. "Maybe, maybe not. I don't know anything about the antiques business."

"Well, you've got to admit it's kind of suspicious," Elizabeth said eagerly.

Amy rolled her eyes. "Oh, no you don't. I thought your mother took all your Amanda Howard books away from you."

"She did." Elizabeth grinned. "But I got one out of the school library today. I have it here in the side pocket of my . . . oh no!"

"What's the matter?" Maria asked.

"It's not here. It must have fallen out. Wait here," she told her friends. "I'll run up to the studio and get it."

Elizabeth ran back inside and hurried up the stairs. As she was about to turn and head into the studio, she noticed that the office door was open. *I know I shouldn't,* she thought. *But I just can't help myself.*

Elizabeth tiptoed right up to the door. There were voices coming from inside the office. She recognized Mr. Beaumont's voice, but not that of the woman talking to him.

Elizabeth listened for another few moments, and then realized with a shock that the female voice belonged to Mrs. Beaumont. But she didn't have an accent anymore!

"We're all set," Mrs. Beaumont was saying. "Our guests arrive at six-thirty. Richard will meet you with the van at six-forty-five." She laughed. "You can clean them out while they're enjoying the second course."

Mr. Beaumont chuckled. "It shouldn't take us too long. The girls provided us with a pretty good idea of who has what and where it is. But after sifting through all the information we've been able to gather about the houses, I've narrowed it down to these. And I say we start with this one." There was a rustling of some papers.

"Definitely," Mrs. Beaumont agreed. "That place is a treasure house. If you run short on time, just hit that one and don't bother with the others. There's enough in that house alone to make it all worthwhile."

"I've got to hand it to you, Margaret. This charm school idea was a good one."

"I told you there was a lot of money in Sweet Valley," Mrs. Beaumont said. "This section of California is a gold mine."

"We've cleared out of the gallery all the stuff we want to take with us. The only thing that's worrying me now is that Elizabeth Wakefield," Mr. Beaumont said.

Elizabeth took a deep breath. She heard her heart hammering in her chest.

"Don't worry," Mrs. Beaumont replied. "I've already thought of a way to keep her out of our hair tonight. We'll give her the Mademoiselle Manners Award. That ought to keep her occupied."

Mr. Beaumont chuckled. "Then we're all set."

Elizabeth tiptoed away from the door. When she was out of earshot, she ran down the hall to the stairwell. She took the steps two at a time and came bursting out of the building.

"Did you find the book?" Amy asked.

"Never mind that," Elizabeth said breathlessly, pulling them down the street. "Wait till you hear this."

She repeated the conversation she had just overheard. When she had finished, neither Amy nor Maria said a word.

"Well?" Elizabeth cried. "What are we going to do?"

Maria and Amy exchanged glances.

"I'd better get going," Maria said softly.

"Me, too," Amy said. "My mom's expecting me home."

"Wait a minute!" Elizabeth cried in frustration. "Don't you believe me?"

Amy looked annoyed. "Look, Elizabeth, I don't know why you think you have to keep going with this gag. But just leave us out of it, OK? You've gotten us into enough trouble as it is."

"But they're crooks!" Elizabeth shouted. "What do I have to do to convince you?"

Maria shook her head. "Maybe you should join the drama club or something. It would give you an outlet for your imagination."

"I'm not imagining things," Elizabeth protested.

Maria shrugged. Then she followed Amy over to the bicycle rack. The two girls unlocked their bikes, climbed on, and began to pedal down the street without a backward glance.

What would Christine Davenport do now? Elizabeth wondered. In Amanda Howard's books, Christine's two best friends always believed her. On the other hand, Christine's two best friends had never been teased by Bruce Patman. If they had, they might not be so true-blue, either.

Elizabeth sighed. If she wanted to foil the Beaumonts' plan, it looked as though she was on her own. She unlocked her bike and rode around the corner. She locked it to a lamp post and started walking the rest of the way home. There was a plan forming in the back of Elizabeth's mind. And she might need her bicycle later that night.

"So you're saying the Beaumonts are planning to clean out the Fowlers tonight?" Jessica said.

"That's right." Elizabeth frowned. "Unless they meant the Howells. Or maybe the Ritemans or the Havers. They all have a lot of nice stuff."

"Uh-huh," Jessica said thoughtfully. "And *you're* going to win the Mademoiselle Manners Award?"

"That's right."

"Unless, of course, they meant Amy. Or maybe Maria," Jessica mimicked.

"Jessica! This is serious!"

"Oh, sure. You really expect me to believe you're going to win the Mademoiselle Manners Award even though you goofed around during all the classes and made a big fool out of yourself in front of Mr. Fowler, Mr. Beaumont, and a curator from the Sweet Valley Museum?"

Elizabeth threw up her hands in frustration. "Why won't anybody believe me?"

"Because it's totally unbelievable. Is this some weird way of getting attention or something?" Jessica pulled a purple knit dress from her closet. "I think I'll wear this tonight. Do you think it looks queenly enough?"

Elizabeth snatched the dress out of Jessica's hands. "I'm telling you the truth!" she said urgently.

"And I'm telling you you're crazy," Jessica said. "You started off saying the Beaumonts were in the phony art and antiques business. You couldn't prove that, so now you decide they're burglars. What next? Are you going to accuse them of dognapping? Jaywalking? Or maybe tax evasion?"

Elizabeth tossed the purple dress on Jessica's bed. "Look," she said. "It's pretty unlikely that I would win the Mademoiselle Manners Award, right?"

"I'd say it was downright impossible," Jessica

said, picking up the dress and starting to pull it on.

"So if I did win it, you'd *have* to believe me, right?" Elizabeth demanded.

"I guess so," Jessica said.

"Great," Elizabeth said with a smile of relief. "Then if I do win, here's what we'll do . . ."

Eleven

"I still don't see why I have to go," Steven complained.

"The Beaumonts were very specific about wanting every member of the family to come to the banquet," Mrs. Wakefield said. "I think it's nice that they're encouraging so much family participation. And besides, I told them you would be there."

"Well, if you ask me, Elizabeth and Jessica have been wasting their time. I mean, they don't seem any more charming than they were before."

"Shut up, Steven," Jessica said.

"See what I mean?" Steven said.

Mr. Wakefield chuckled. "Maybe they just don't see any reason to waste all that hard-earned charm on their brother."

Steven rubbed his forehead. "Anyway, I wouldn't mind going that much except that I have this terrible headache," he complained. "I've had it all afternoon and it's getting worse and worse."

Mrs. Wakefield looked concerned. "Why didn't you mention it before?" she asked.

"I don't know," Steven said. "I guess I thought it would go away."

Mr. Wakefield put his hand on Steven's head. "You don't seem to have a fever."

"I think it's a sinus headache," Steven said.

Mrs. Wakefield sighed. "Well, we're certainly not going to force you to go if you're not feeling well. But if we leave you at home, I want you to promise that you'll get into bed and stay there."

"I will," Steven promised. "In fact, I think I'll go lie down right now." He trudged out of the den and started up the stairs.

"You fell for that?" Jessica fumed. "I can't believe you're not going to make him come. It's really rude. The Beaumonts will be expecting him. I think you should at least call and tell them he's not coming."

"That's not necessary. I'm sure they'll understand," Mrs. Wakefield said. "There will be so many people there, they probably won't even notice. Now go finish getting ready or we'll be late."

*   *   *

And they were late. By the time Steven had been settled into bed, Jessica had fixed her hair, and Mr. Wakefield had taken a last-minute phone call from a client, the Wakefields were twenty minutes late starting out for the banquet.

"Hurry," Elizabeth urged as she climbed into the van.

Mr. Wakefield threw her a curious look. "What's the rush? I thought you didn't like charm school."

"I'm hungry," Elizabeth explained weakly.

It was almost seven by the time they arrived. "Here we are," Mr. Wakefield said as he parked the van on the street across from the charm school building. "Looks pretty crowded. We were lucky to find a parking space."

Elizabeth and Jessica climbed out of the back seat. Mrs. Wakefield smiled at them. "You both look very pretty." Then she frowned. "But why are you bringing your backpack, Elizabeth? It doesn't really go with your nice dress. Don't you want to leave it in the van?"

Elizabeth froze. She needed that backpack. And she didn't feel like explaining why.

"Ah . . . um . . . the hot rollers are in it," Elizabeth said with a sudden burst of inspiration. "Jessica thought she might need them in case the crown flattens down her hair."

Mr. Wakefield smiled. "Still counting on winning the Mademoiselle Manners Award, Jessica?"

"I know I'm going to win it," she said confidently. "Even though *some* people have certain other crazy ideas."

"Now, Jessica," Mrs. Wakefield cautioned, "if Janet Howell does win, I want you to promise me you'll be a good sport about it."

Elizabeth and Jessica shared a meaningful glance. "Sure, Mom. Don't worry," Jessica said.

The Wakefields hurried across the street and into the building. "You guys go on in," Jessica instructed her parents when they'd reached the second floor. "Elizabeth and I are supposed to meet the other girls in the office."

Mr. Wakefield nodded. "Good luck with the contest, girls. We'll see you inside." He and Mrs. Wakefield headed into the studio.

The twins hurried down the hall toward the office. "I'll meet you there," Elizabeth told her sister. "I've got to stash this first."

Jessica rolled her eyes. "Whatever you say. But just for the record, I still think you're crazy."

Elizabeth ducked into the ladies' room and stuffed her backpack down behind a large trash can. Then she rushed down the hall to the office.

She was the last one to arrive. All the other girls were crowded in, whispering and giggling.

"Well, if it isn't Amanda Howard," Janet Howell said with a laugh when she noticed Elizabeth come in.

She won't be laughing tomorrow, Elizabeth thought. But all she said was, "Hi, Janet." She scanned the room for Amy and Maria. When she spotted them on the other side of the room, they both looked away, refusing to meet her eye. *I just hope they'll be there when I need them*, Elizabeth thought. *Maybe I'd better try to talk to them.*

She had just started moving through the crowd when Mrs. Beaumont appeared at the door wearing a blue chiffon dress and a worried expression. When she saw the twins, her face relaxed. "Here you are," she exclaimed, sounding relieved. "We've been waiting for you."

"Wow!" Jessica said. "What a gorgeous dress!"

Mrs. Beaumont smiled at the girls. "And how beautiful you all look!"

Elizabeth noticed that Mrs. Beaumont's accent was back.

"I won't keep you in suspense," Mrs. Beaumont continued. "I know how eager you are to know who will be our Queen this evening." She produced the glittering tiara from behind her back. "So without further ado, the moment you've all been waiting for . . ."

"I hope you've been practicing your curtsy," Elizabeth heard Jessica whisper to Janet. "You're going to be doing it a lot."

"The winner of the Mademoiselle Manners Award, and tonight's Queen of Charm, is . . ." Mrs. Beaumont smiled and looked at each girl, prolonging the suspense. "Mademoiselle Elizabeth Wakefield!" she announced.

There were gasps and surprised exclamations from the other students.

Mrs. Beaumont held up her hand for silence. "I know my choice may come as a surprise to some of you," she said. "But I am awarding this honor to Mademoiselle Elizabeth because I think that she has made the most progress in the shortest amount of time. Surely you won't begrudge her this little moment in the sun. Come, Elizabeth. Receive your crown."

"But it's not fair!" Jessica wailed loudly. Then, bursting into loud sobs, she pushed past Mrs. Beaumont and ran from the room.

The office erupted into excited whispers.

Elizabeth gave Mrs. Beaumont an apologetic smile. "You'll have to forgive Jessica. She's very disappointed. Let me go talk to her for just a moment. Then I'll come back to accept my crown."

Mrs. Beaumont frowned. "Yes. Well, please hurry, then. Everyone is waiting."

"I'll hurry," Elizabeth promised.

Jessica was already undressed when Elizabeth rushed into the ladies' room.

Elizabeth grinned at her twin. "You were great," she said, peeling off her pink party dress and handing it to Jessica. "I almost believed you were really upset."

Jessica stepped into the pink dress while Elizabeth fished her backpack out from behind the trash can and pulled out a sweater and a pair of jeans.

"I *am* upset," Jessica said. "I can't believe I actually knocked myself out trying to win that stupid award, when the whole thing was fixed! Do you know how many hours I spent walking around with a dictionary on my head?"

Elizabeth giggled. "Well, you have one consolation—at least Janet didn't win, either."

"You were right about the Beaumonts, though," Jessica exclaimed. "I can't believe it. But you were right."

"I'm just glad you believed me." Elizabeth

handed Jessica the ribbon from her hair and the pink bracelet she had been wearing. Then she pulled on her jeans and zipped them. "Amy and Maria thought I was imagining the whole thing. Jess, you've got to convince them to help me. I may need them if anything goes wrong."

"I'll try," Jessica promised. She slipped the bracelet on her wrist and then looked in the mirror. She grinned. "I look so much like you, I could be your twin!"

Elizabeth stuffed the clothes that Jessica had been wearing into the backpack. Then she buried the backpack in the trash can under a bunch of paper towels. "Very funny," she said, trying not to smile. "Now come on, let's go."

Jessica paused and gave her sister a worried look. "Are you sure you know what you're doing?"

Elizabeth smiled. "Are you kidding? I didn't read all those Amanda Howard books for nothing."

A moment later, Jessica walked into the office and smiled. "Jessica is a little upset. She wants us to go ahead without her."

Mrs. Beaumont frowned. "Perhaps I should go and talk to her."

"No, that would just make it worse. She

needs some time alone. She was really counting on winning this award," Jessica said. "And I must say, I think she's the one who really deserved it," she couldn't resist adding.

Mrs. Beaumont waved her hand impatiently, as if she didn't care one way or the other. "Yes, well, we must try to get back on schedule. We are running late." She plopped the tiara unceremoniously on Jessica's head. "Line up," she ordered the girls.

"Aren't you going to make a little coronation speech or something?" Jessica asked, feeling disappointed.

"We really don't have time," Mrs. Beaumont snapped. "Now let me just do a head count."

Jessica nervously turned, searching out Maria and Amy. She saw them looking at her suspiciously. She hurried toward them.

"Elizabeth?" Amy asked tentatively.

Jessica shook her head slightly. "Jessica," she said under her breath.

"I thought so," Amy said. "What's going on? Where's Elizabeth?"

Jessica looked around to make sure no one else was listening. She leaned closer to Amy and Maria. "It's a long story," she whispered. "But here's what she wants you to do. One of you has to be at the pay phone by the ladies' room every twenty minutes starting at seven-twenty. If Elizabeth *doesn't* call, it means she's in trouble."

"Mademoiselle Elizabeth," Mrs. Beaumont called out. "Come to the head of the line, please."

Jessica turned away but Amy grabbed her sleeve. "But where is Elizabeth?" she demanded in a whisper.

"On a stakeout," Jessica answered. She straightened her tiara and walked to the front of the line.

Twelve

Elizabeth hid in the stall until she heard a burst of applause. She knew that meant the students had entered the studio and the banquet had started.

Elizabeth shoved her flashlight into her pocket and moved noiselessly toward the door. She opened it a crack and peeked out. The hall was empty.

She slipped out of the ladies' room. Pausing for a moment at the pay phone, she memorized the number before silently descending the stairs.

It was dark outside by this time, and Elizabeth glanced around nervously as she walked toward her bicycle. It was funny how eerie and dangerous the street seemed when there were no shoppers or pedestrians around.

Elizabeth's hands were shaking as she fumbled with the lock on her bicycle. *Calm down,* she told herself firmly. *Remember, Christine Davenport always keeps a cool head.* She took some deep breaths until her hands stopped shaking. Then she climbed on her bicycle and rode off into the dark night.

There were no lights on in the Fowler mansion. Elizabeth parked her bicycle behind a hedge across the street and settled down to wait.

I've got to catch them in the act, she thought. *As soon as I see them break into the house, I'll call the police. Then they'll race over here and catch Mr. Beaumont and Richard red-handed.*

She looked up and down the street. She was sure that the Fowler mansion was the treasure house the Beaumonts had mentioned. The Fowlers were the richest family in town. So where was the white van? Could they have been there already?

Elizabeth snuck out from behind the hedge and hurried across the street and over the front lawn. She peeked into the front windows. Even without lights, she could tell that nothing had been disturbed.

Suddenly, a light went on in the living room.

Elizabeth quickly ducked her head. Then, very slowly, she raised it again to look inside.

It was Mrs. Pervis. Elizabeth watched as the housekeeper cleared some coffee cups off a side table, then turned off the lights and left the room.

Just then Elizabeth heard the sound of an engine. She turned and caught her breath. *It was the white van!*

They're coming! Elizabeth thought. *But what about Mrs. Pervis? Should I warn her?*

By now the van was right in front of the house. But to Elizabeth's surprise, it didn't even slow down. It drove right by the house and turned the corner.

They're not coming here, Elizabeth realized. *They must know that the Fowlers have servants. I'll bet they're going to the Howells'.*

Elizabeth ran across the street, grabbed her bicycle, and began to pedal as fast as she could toward the Howells' house.

"Maria," Mrs. Slater said, "I'm glad to see that your table manners have improved dramatically."

They were just finishing their salads. Maria had demonstrated what she had learned by instructing her sister on which of the many forks to use.

Maria looked at her watch. "Yes, I've really been working hard to improve them," she said absently. "Would you excuse me, please?"

Maria got up and hurried out of the room. She knew it was rude, and she'd probably get in trouble for it later. *I just hope it's for a good cause,* she thought.

When she stepped into the hallway, the pay phone was already ringing. She rushed over to it and grabbed the receiver off the hook. "Hello?" she said breathlessly.

"It's me," she heard Elizabeth say. "I'm at the pay phone at the little shopping strip on Wellington Street."

"What's going on, Elizabeth? Are you all right?" Maria blinked as Jessica came running down the hall and whisked into the ladies' room.

"I don't have time to talk," Elizabeth said quickly. "But I was wrong. They're not hitting the Fowlers' house. So I'm heading over to the Howells'."

"Elizabeth," Maria pleaded, "if you really think there's something going on, you should call the police."

"I will," Elizabeth promised. "Just as soon as I catch them in the act."

The ladies' room door opened again, and Jessica came charging out. This time, she was wearing the purple dress.

"Hold it!" shouted Maria. Jessica skidded to a stop.

"What's wrong?" Elizabeth asked.

"Not you," Maria said into the phone. With her free hand, Maria frantically pointed to the tiara on Jessica's head.

"Oops," Jessica said. She ducked back into the ladies' room.

"I see the van," Elizabeth said excitedly. "I've got to go. I'll call again in twenty minutes."

Jessica emerged from the ladies' room without the crown and ran toward the studio door.

Maria hung up the phone and followed Jessica into the banquet hall. She paused for a moment at Amy's table. "Elizabeth just called," she whispered in Amy's ear. "They're not hitting the Fowlers', so she's on her way to the Howells'."

"I'll take the next shift," Amy whispered back. "Do you really think she's on to something?"

Maria shook her head in dismay. "I don't know. But I sure hope she knows what she's doing."

"Jessica!" Mrs. Wakefield exclaimed. "Where have you been? And where is Elizabeth?"

"Elizabeth wanted a few minutes in private to compose her speech," Jessica said. "I think she's down the hall in the office. And I've been in the bathroom . . . um . . . crying."

Mrs. Wakefield patted her hand. "I know

you're upset about not winning, sweetie. But you have to be a good sport about these things."

"Sure, Mom," Jessica replied, relieved. Usually their parents could tell the twins apart even when they were trying to look like each other. Luckily, the Wakefields were seated near Brooke Dennis and her father. Mr. Dennis had been keeping Mr. and Mrs. Wakefield so captivated with his tales of Hollywood that they hadn't noticed that Jessica was playing both twins.

I just hope they stay distracted long enough for Elizabeth to complete her plan, Jessica thought grimly. *Otherwise we're both in big trouble!*

Elizabeth pedaled hard toward the Howells' house. Making the phone call had taken her out of her way, but she hoped that wouldn't matter. If her calculations were correct, the robbery should be in progress when she arrived.

The Howells lived only a few blocks from the Wakefields, and in order to get there, Elizabeth had to bicycle by her own house. She glanced at it as she rode by and saw that the lights were on upstairs. From the street she could hear the sound of Steven's stereo blasting out of his window. *For somebody with a headache, he sure is playing his music loudly,* she thought wryly.

As she left her house behind there was a flash

of light behind her. She maneuvered her bike up onto the sidewalk and watched as the white van passed by and turned at the corner.

She pedaled even harder. But there was no sign of the van when Elizabeth turned the corner herself and pulled up in front of the Howells' house. She parked her bike across the street and waited. But by the time she had to find a phone and check in again, the white van still hadn't turned up.

"Hello?" Amy said into the phone, glancing up and down the charm school hallway.

"You guys are doing great," she heard Elizabeth say.

"Believe me, it's not easy," Amy retorted.

Jessica hurried past her and disappeared into the ladies' room.

"Maria and I can't keep coming up with excuses to leave the table all night. And Jessica's popping in and out of the ladies' room like a jackrabbit."

"I know. I know," Elizabeth said.

"So have they done anything incriminating yet?"

Elizabeth sighed. "Not yet. But I know they will. I'm going to check the Ritemans' house next."

"Elizabeth, are you sure—" Amy began.

"Listen, I've got to go," Elizabeth interrupted. "I'll talk to you or Maria in twenty minutes."

"OK. Good luck." Amy stood there for a moment after Elizabeth had hung up the phone, nervously chewing on her fingernail.

Jessica came back out of the bathroom dressed like Elizabeth—complete with tiara. "Well?" she asked.

Amy shook her head. "She hasn't seen anything yet. Now how are you going to explain Jessica's disappearance?"

"Simple," Jessica replied. "I'll just say that Jessica turned out to be a bad sport and she couldn't stand to hear me, *Elizabeth*, give my acceptance speech."

Amy grinned. "Yeah. That sounds pretty plausible."

"Well, thanks," Jessica said sarcastically.

"I didn't mean it that way," Amy said quickly. She put her hand on Jessica's arm. "You do think Elizabeth will be all right, don't you?"

Jessica shrugged. "I've been too busy changing clothes to think about it," she said, hurrying off toward the banquet hall.

Thirteen

◇

When Elizabeth reached the Ritemans' house, the van wasn't there.

It must be the Havers', then, she thought, turning her bicycle. *Please be the Havers'. Please! If nothing happens, I'll never live it down. I'll be a complete laughingstock.*

But when she got to the Havers', the van wasn't there, either. What's more, she realized it was time to check in again.

Why didn't I say every thirty minutes? she thought in frustration. *I'll go home and call. It's closer than the pay phone. And if I sneak in the back door, Steven won't even know I'm there.*

Elizabeth parked her bicycle behind a neighbor's hedge. She noticed that the upstairs lights were off now, and the house was quiet. But the front porch lights were on, and she saw Steven standing at the front door with Bob Lesko, one of his basketball teammates. Steven turned to lock the door.

Elizabeth crept forward, staying in the shadows.

"We can't stay long," she heard Steven say. "I'm supposed to be home with a sinus headache. I had to fake it to get out of going to some dumb charm school banquet with my sisters."

"We'll be back in an hour," Bob assured him. "But we've got to get over there to see the Springfield team practice tonight. I want to get a look at their talent before we go up against them next week."

Suddenly Elizabeth saw headlights approaching. She stepped back behind a bush and put her hand over her mouth to stifle a gasp. The white van was coming down the street, moving very slowly.

"Cool van," Bob commented. "I wonder whose it is?"

"I don't know," Steven answered. "But I saw it go by about four times while I was waiting for you."

Steven put his keys in his pocket and the two boys headed off down the street. Meanwhile, Elizabeth saw the van turn the corner at the end of the block and disappear.

Elizabeth hurried to the back door and let herself into the kitchen. *I'd better leave the lights off in case Steven comes back for something*, she thought.

She picked up the phone and began to dial.

"Excuse me," Maria said suddenly. She started to rise from her seat.

"Are you ill?" Mrs. Slater asked, a note of irritation in her voice.

"No, I just . . . um . . . need to wash my hands."

"Sweetheart, it's very rude to keep getting up and leaving," Mrs. Slater protested.

"I'm sorry," Maria said breathlessly. "I just have to."

"Maria!" Mrs. Slater exclaimed.

But Maria was already out the door and running toward the phone. It started to ring just as she reached it. She grabbed the receiver off the hook. "Where are you?" she demanded.

"I'm home," Elizabeth answered.

"Whose home?"

"*My* home," Elizabeth said.

"What are you doing *there*?"

"Calling you," Elizabeth replied impatiently.

"Elizabeth, my mom is ready to kill me,"

Maria said. "How much longer do we have to keep this up?"

Elizabeth ignored the question. "I'm going to the Ritemans'," she told Maria. "I'll call you when—*oh! Oh no!*" Elizabeth's voice broke off abruptly.

"Elizabeth?" Maria said. "Are you there? Elizabeth? Is something wrong?"

There was a click. And then Maria heard a dial tone.

Elizabeth struggled as hard as she could, but the hand that was clamped over her mouth was like iron. Another strong arm was wrapped around her, pinning her arms at her sides.

She let herself go limp, and the hand over her mouth briefly relaxed. Elizabeth seized the opportunity.

"Ouch!" Mr. Beaumont yelled as Elizabeth bit down on his hand. He dropped her to the floor and she rolled toward the kitchen door, determined to escape.

"Oh, no you don't," Richard said, grabbing her by the ankle.

The next thing Elizabeth knew, she was being shoved into the broom closet. Her captors slammed the door shut and turned the key in the lock.

"Is Margaret crazy or what?" she heard Richard say angrily. "This house was supposed to be empty. We've spent most of the evening driving around the neighborhood waiting for the boy to leave, and now we find one of those twins here. What's going on?"

"I don't know," Mr. Beaumont said. "But relax. We can take the kid with us. Might be a good insurance policy until we're safely across the Mexican border."

"I don't know," Richard said doubtfully. "She sure manages to make a lot of trouble."

Mr. Beaumont laughed nastily. "Mostly for herself. Now let's get started. We're not going to have time to hit any other houses."

Richard chuckled. "That's OK. There's enough loot in this place to set us up for life."

"You're right. We really hit the jackpot with this one," Mr. Beaumont said. "Margaret should be sneaking out of the banquet about now. She'll meet us across the border. Then it's *au revoir*, Beaumonts. *Hola*, Señor and Señora Diaz. We set up shop in Mexico and do the whole scam again."

Richard laughed. "I just hope we have enough room in the van for all the Wakefield valuables."

Wakefield valuables? Elizabeth thought. She would have laughed if she hadn't been so frightened. *If they think Mom's antique jewelry is going to set them up for life, they're going to be very disappointed.* She felt around on the closet floor until she located the old tennis shoe where Mrs. Wakefield's heirlooms were hidden, and clutched it to her chest.

Amy and Maria had summoned Jessica to the back of the banquet room for a quick conference. "Level with us," Maria begged. "This was all some kind of elaborate practical joke, right?"

"No! What do you mean?" Jessica demanded. "Didn't Elizabeth call?"

"She called," Maria whispered. "She said she was at your house. Then she made some kind of noise like she was in trouble and hung up. It's got to be a joke. Why would they be robbing your house when they could be robbing the Fowlers' place or the Howells'? It doesn't make any sense."

"I don't know." Jessica frowned, thinking hard.

Then it hit her, and she felt a terrible weight in the pit of her stomach. Of course they were at her house! They thought the Wakefields had tons of stuff worth stealing. *Because that's what I told them!*

"Call the police!" Jessica cried. "Call them *now!*"

Amy and Maria looked startled for a moment,

but Jessica's panicky voice seemed to convince them. They ran out of the room.

Jessica was about to follow them when she saw Mrs. Beaumont step up to the podium at the front of the room. *This is my chance,* she thought grimly. *If she and her sneaky partners have done anything to hurt Elizabeth, I'll make sure they don't get away with it!*

Mrs. Beaumont tapped the microphone to make sure it was turned on. "And now," she said with a dazzling smile, "I believe our Queen of Charm has a few words to say."

Mrs. Beaumont stepped down, and Jessica went hurrying toward the front, stumbling on the hem of Elizabeth's skirt as she went. She stepped up to the podium and looked out over the sea of faces. What could she say?

Then, out of the corner of her eye, she saw Mrs. Beaumont moving surreptitiously toward the door. Jessica took a deep breath. "Stop her!" she shouted into the microphone. She pointed to Mrs. Beaumont. "She's a crook and a phony. And her creepy husband has done something to my sister!"

A gasp went up from the surprised onlookers. A few seconds later, most of the girls began to giggle.

Jessica could see her father jump up and rush

toward her. His face was furious. *"Elizabeth Wakefield!"* he thundered. "Enough is enough!"

Jessica looked over and saw that Janet was laughing so hard, she could barely stand. Jessica grabbed the microphone again. "And for your information, Janet Howell, it's me, *Jessica*. Not Elizabeth!"

The laugh froze on Janet's face. Mr. Wakefield took Jessica by the arm.

"I *told* you I'd wind up as the Queen of Charm," Jessica shouted at Janet.

She just managed to stick her tongue out at Janet before her father yanked her off the podium.

Inside the broom closet, Elizabeth was shaking.

"I don't understand it," she heard Richard say. "This house is supposed to be stuffed with art and antiques."

"Let's ask the kid. Maybe her folks were more suspicious than they let on," Mr. Beaumont said. "They could have hidden everything."

Suddenly the closet door was yanked open and Mr. Beaumont and Richard loomed over Elizabeth.

"OK," Mr. Beaumont said. "Where's the stuff?"

"What stuff?" Elizabeth asked.

"You know what stuff. The valuable stuff your parents have hidden."

Wordlessly, Elizabeth offered them the old tennis shoe.

Mr. Beaumont's eyes narrowed. He took a step forward. Then he froze.

"Sirens!" Richard hissed.

Elizabeth gasped. She heard sirens, too. And they were getting louder.

"Let's get out of here," Richard said. He shoved the closet door shut and locked it again.

"Wait!" Elizabeth cried.

Then she heard the most comforting sound she could imagine: *"Hold it! Police!"*

Fourteen

"Elizabeth Wakefield, don't you ever do anything like that again!" Mrs. Wakefield's voice was simultaneously shaky and angry, and she was hugging Elizabeth as hard as she could.

"I'm very proud of you for figuring things out and being persistent," Mr. Wakefield said. "But don't *ever* put yourself in this kind of danger again. There's no painting or antique desk in the world worth risking your safety for."

Mrs. Wakefield turned to Jessica. "And as for you, why didn't you tell us what was going on?"

"Because you wouldn't have believed me any more than you did Elizabeth," Jessica said. "Probably less, in fact."

The twins and their parents were standing in their front yard. Mr. Beaumont and Richard had been handcuffed and were now being loaded into the back of a police car. Several other squad cars were parked nearby, their lights flashing. The Wakefields' van was still in the middle of the front yard, where Mr. Wakefield had driven in his haste. Many of the neighbors had come out of their houses to see what was going on.

At that moment a solitary figure came walking down the street and then froze. "Holy cow!"

They all looked up and saw Steven, who was staring at the bizarre scene with his mouth wide open.

"Steven!" Mr. Wakefield exclaimed.

Steven gulped. "I was only gone for an hour. You didn't have to call the police!"

The twins looked at each other and grinned.

The next day at school, Amy, Maria, and Elizabeth discovered that they were heroes.

"I saw your pictures in the paper," Aaron Dallas said as he joined the crowd that had gathered around the three girls before homeroom.

"Who didn't?" Winston Egbert said, laughing. "They were on the front page."

"So, Elizabeth," Melissa McCormick asked eagerly. "Why did those Beaumont characters bother with the antiques and art business?"

"It helped them to figure out who had a lot

of money and would be likely to have stuff worth stealing," Elizabeth explained. "They had a few things that would attract the right kind of target. When they delivered them, they were able to get into people's houses and check them out—find out if the families had alarm systems or live-in maids."

"So are they really Swiss or what?" Kerry Glenn asked.

"Mrs. Beaumont isn't. She actually lived in Sweet Valley a long time ago. She went to high school with my mom. But she must have met her husband in Europe somewhere. The police are still trying to figure out who Mr. Beaumont and Richard are. They both have about a zillion passports and aliases. Apparently they've pulled this scam all over the world. Their next stop was supposed to be Mexico."

"Wow," Kerry said, impressed. "It's amazing that you guys were able to foil a gang of infamous international criminals. Congratulations."

Elizabeth smiled. "Thanks, Kerry."

"Yeah, congratulations, Elizabeth. It was really smart of you to figure out their plan," added Sarah Thomas.

Todd Wilkins stepped forward. He and Elizabeth had known each other since kindergarten, and lately they had become closer than ever. Elizabeth liked to think of Todd as her sort-of boyfriend. They hadn't been on a real date yet, but he had kissed her once. "Congratulations from me, too, Elizabeth," Todd said softly. "I'm really glad you're safe."

Elizabeth smiled up at Todd. "Thank you, Todd," she replied. *Now I know how Christine Davenport must feel when she cracks a tough case*, she thought happily. *And I like it.*

After four periods of praise and admiration, Elizabeth, Maria, and Amy collapsed at a table in the lunchroom. As Elizabeth was unwrapping her tuna sandwich she looked up and saw Amy and Maria grinning at her from across the table.

"Sorry we doubted you," Amy said.

"We should have known you wouldn't have made up anything like that," Maria said penitently.

"That's OK," Elizabeth said with a smile. "The important thing is that you came through for me when I needed you. And that's what friends are supposed to do."

The three of them raised their milk cartons for a toast, and then burst into laughter.

Just then Patty Gilbert walked by and didn't

even give them a smile. She had her ballet slippers slung over her shoulder and a sullen look on her face.

Amy watched her disappear in the direction of the gym. "Speaking of friends, why do you suppose Patty is so determined not to have any? After English today I asked her if she wanted to write an article on ballet for *The Sixers* and she totally snubbed me. From what I hear, that's how she treats everybody."

"Maybe she's shy," Elizabeth suggested.

Maria shook her head. "She's not shy. She's driven. Believe me, I know the type. Hollywood is full of kids like that. They have a dream and they're not going to let anything get in the way. Having friends takes too much time."

"That's a shame," Elizabeth said, staring after Patty thoughtfully. "Because she seems like a girl with a lot to offer."

What will it take to make Patty Gilbert realize how important friends are? Find out in Sweet Valley Twins and Friends #65, PATTY'S LAST DANCE.